*"Why Pretend?"*

"Why deny what you know you want? Surely this isn't the first time—"

Connie's hand flew toward his cheek but was easily intercepted.

"Isn't that gesture just a shade Victorian?" His voice was bitter, mocking.

"Perhaps, but then you're behaving rather like a Victorian villain." Enraged, she managed to wrench her hand from his iron grasp. "And suppose you tell me just what there would be for me in such an arrangement?"

"Pleasure."

Then he was kissing her, gently but skillfully, his lips touching her eyes, her lips. . . .

---

MARY LEE STANLEY
and her husband have traveled all over Western Europe. For a while, they lived in Aix-en-Provence and now divide their time between Gramercy Park and their studio in Paris. The setting of her first Silhouette romance reflects her love for southern France.

Dear Reader:

I'd like to take this opportunity to thank you for all your support and encouragement of Silhouette Romances.

Many of you write in regularly, telling us what you like best about Silhouette, which authors are your favorites. This is a tremendous help to us as we strive to publish the best contemporary romances possible.

All the romances from Silhouette Books are for you, so enjoy this book and the many stories to come. I hope you'll continue to share your thoughts with us, and invite you to write to us at the address below:

Karen Solem
Editor-in-Chief
Silhouette Books
P.O. Box 769
New York, N.Y. 10019

# MARY LEE STANLEY

# No Trifling With Love

*Silhouette* *Romance*

Published by Silhouette Books New York

**America's Publisher of Contemporary Romance**

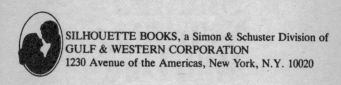

SILHOUETTE BOOKS, a Simon & Schuster Division of
GULF & WESTERN CORPORATION
1230 Avenue of the Americas, New York, N.Y. 10020

ISBN: 0-671-57183-4

First Silhouette Books printing October, 1982

10 9 8 7 6 5 4 3 2 1

Map by Ray Lundgren

Once more to S.E.M.

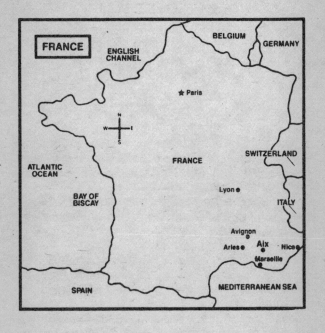

# Chapter One

"Which side does the tassel go on, Marge?" Connie Wyatt asked, as she tilted the mortarboard at a rakish angle and studied her reflection in the mirror she shared with her college roommate.

"At the back before you get your degree, to the right after, I think is what Dean Lewis told us. Or was it the other way around?"

"You're a big help, I must say."

"Always glad to oblige." Marjorie Hamilton stood next to Connie at the mirror. "I look like a giant crow in this getup." She spread her arms and flapped the graduation gown.

Connie looked at her with amusement for a moment, then her expression grew serious. "Can you believe we're actually going to graduate tomorrow? Somehow I guess I thought school would never end—that it would just go on forever."

"That's what my father said every time he paid the tuition." Marjorie laughed. "And speaking of fathers, aren't your parents due in soon?"

"Actually, they were supposed to be here a few hours ago. But you know Mother. She probably made

Dad turn around fifty miles out of Baltimore to make sure she hadn't left the oven on."

"Doesn't that just drive you crazy? Remember the time—" Marjorie broke off at the sight of Dean Ann Lewis framed in the doorway, her face grave.

"Connie . . ." Dean Lewis seemed strangely hesitant.

"Don't tell me." Connie groaned. "The gym department didn't record those credits after all."

"I wish it were no more than that, Connie."

"Should I leave, Dean Lewis?" Marjorie asked.

"No, Marjorie, I think it would be best if you stayed. Connie—I have some very terrible news . . . I don't even know how to tell you . . . My dear, I've just had a call from the Essex police. There's been an accident. Your parents . . ."

"They're hurt!"

"No, Connie. It's worse than that. I'm afraid they're both dead."

Connie was aware of the sun's heat on her back as she mounted the two steps to the walkway leading to the brown and white frame house on Roland Avenue. Idly she paused to look up at the cloudless blue sky and realized with a shock that this was the first time she had been conscious of whether the day was gray or bright since that dreadful morning three weeks before.

Steeling herself against the terrible surge of grief that constricted her throat at the sight of the house, her home for her entire life up to now, she stood for a moment, incapable of moving, and found herself staring at the wrought-iron sign—C. W. Wyatt—that had been on the lawn as long as she could remember. As she bent down and pried it loose from the neglected grass, she was struck by the symbolism; it was the first of many marks of her parents that she would have to remove for whoever would take possession of the house now that they were gone.

"Connie!" The voice came from the side yard next door, and Ann Bennett, her plump face shielded from the sun by a large, floppy gardening hat, came hurrying over, immediately encircling Connie in her ample embrace. Ann had been her mother's closest friend, and, because the Bennetts had no children, they had lavished all their love on Connie, making her feel that she had a second home during the years when she was growing up and going to school in Baltimore.

Ann wept as she said, "Connie, Connie, it's just so awful. I still can't believe it." Continuing to pat her gently, she added, "I loved them too, you know."

Connie stoically submitted to Ann's weepy efforts to console her. Though her own heart was still heavy, she felt the time for tears was over; the past would always be with her, but it was important that she turn her attention to the future. Paradoxically she found herself comforting Ann Bennett. "I know you did. I meant to call you before I came over today, but I guess I wasn't sure I could go through with this. I've been putting it off for days now."

"Putting what off?" Ann asked, puzzled.

"I think I'm going to rent the house for a while, at least until I have some idea of what I'm going to do, where I want to go—all the things I can't seem to decide on at the moment . . ."

Ann first looked at Connie in sympathetic silence, then, as though seeing her for the first time, with a sharp intake of breath and an almost visible surprise.

"Oh, Connie, you're really grown up now, aren't you? I guess I've kept thinking of you as the little girl who used to stop by every afternoon after school for cookies." Instead, before her stood an exceptionally attractive young woman. Although Connie's arresting blue-violet eyes were rimmed by fatigue and her thick, tawny-chestnut hair was tied back carelessly with a simple ribbon, not even her great grief and her obvious complete indifference to the way she looked could hide the radiant complexion or the woman's body under the simple blue shirtwaist dress.

Connie's generous mouth was set in a determined line as she said to Ann, "I'm afraid I need more than cookies now—though there have been plenty of times in the last few weeks when I've wished I could go back to being that carefree child," she added with a wry smile.

Ann nodded sympathetically. "You know, dear, you have to give yourself time to take it all in. It would be a mistake to make any decisions just yet. Actually, Tom and I had hoped you would stay with us, at least until you get your bearings. Though I can see that being next door to home might be hard for you, and if you don't want to, we'll certainly understand. Just as long as you realize that you're welcome to stay for however long you want. No one knows better than you," she sighed wistfully, "how much room we have and how much we'd love to have you. And of course you'd be free to come and go as you pleased."

Connie gave Ann a warm hug and the best smile she could manage. "Thanks, Ann. I appreciate that, but I'm with the Hamiltons now—you remember Marjorie Hamilton, don't you—and I might as well stay put." Then, as if realizing how ungracious that must seem, she nervously added, forgetting that Ann Bennett knew very well where the Hamiltons lived, "They're just four blocks down Roland Avenue, so it's convenient—"

She broke off abruptly, overcome by a rush of feeling as she remembered how for years she had stopped every day to pick up Marjorie on her way to Whittier, the girls' school they had both attended. Their friendship had survived all this time: they had gone on to the same college, even roomed together. It was Marjorie who had been her mainstay when the news came about her parents; Marjorie and her family who had somehow managed everything for her while she went, like an automaton, through the funeral; the Hamiltons who had picked up her diploma, packed her things, and all but carried her back to Baltimore, ensconcing her in their house and surrounding her with their love. And now it was Ed Hamilton, Marjorie's father, who was helping her settle the details of the estate.

"Well, dear," Ann sighed, "I suppose you know best. Just remember, though—you're welcome here whenever you want and for as long as you want." Then, suddenly noticing the nameplate Connie had set down on the ground, she asked, "What are you going to do with *that?*"

For a moment Connie didn't know what Ann was talking about. She had completely forgotten the forlorn object lying at her feet.

"I don't know," she replied, fighting back the tears that threatened to flow despite all her efforts. "I don't know what I'm going to do about anything just yet! Mr. Hamilton told me about someone who wants an immediate rental—and a furnished one, at that—so I thought I should at least speak to the man. Apparently his house burned down, and he and his daughter need a place to stay. It occurred to me that I'd better clear out some personal things, just put some stuff into one room and lock it all up. I guess I just started off with this." She picked up the nameplate, held it at arm's length, and looked at it; then she said, her voice firm, "I'm going to rent the house for the next year. By then I should know what I want to do."

11

Ann's interest was aroused. "Did Ed Hamilton tell you who this man was?"

"Yes, of course he did." Then teasingly Connie added, "Actually I got quite a rundown. According to Mr. Hamilton, he's been the prime mover in the harbor restoration project and on the board of just about everything, including the Baltimore Symphony. To top it all off, he's from an 'old and well-to-do family'—those are Mr. Hamilton's words, not mine. Frankly, he sounds horribly stodgy and proper to me."

"Um-hm." Ann nodded knowingly. "Say no more. George Trevelyan. Although *proper* is the very last word I'd use to describe him."

"You make him sound so sinister! Do you think he's the kind of man who'll abscond with the silver or fail to pay the rent?" Connie laughed, then added curiously, "How did you guess who it was?"

"The minute you mentioned the house burning down, I knew it would have to be George Trevelyan. It was before your—before your graduation, and I guess you wouldn't have heard, but there was quite a to-do about it." Ann Bennett's eyes narrowed. "It was rather horrible, you know. He and his daughter, Diana, got out of the house, but Mrs. Trevelyan didn't. The fire spread *very* rapidly, and no one ever learned exactly what had happened." Ann's voice trailed off, then she added, almost reluctantly: "You know, Connie, I don't like to gossip, but there were a lot of rumors going around about George Trevelyan."

"Are you suggesting that I have to worry about arson if he rents from me?" Connie asked half-jokingly.

"I wasn't talking about the fire, Connie," Ann replied almost sharply. "What I meant was that everybody knew that George Trevelyan was insanely jealous of his wife—never let her out of his sight—though I

12

must say, if he was, he had no right to be! He himself was supposed to have had a few affairs. All very discreet, of course, but still, imagine the arrogance of the man! Anyhow, the fire gave rise to a lot of talk about their relationship not having been as perfect as it seemed."

"Even if it wasn't—how awful to throw it up at him after such a terrible accident! Besides, if he was jealous of her, it must have meant that he loved her. Imagine what he must have felt when he wasn't able to save her!"

Connie was shocked, but she was also interested. For the first time in weeks, she realized, she was aware of something besides her own loss, and though she dismissed the whole story of jealousy and infidelity as too melodramatic to be real, her curiosity about the Trevelyans was aroused.

Eager to know more, she tried another approach. "Mr. Hamilton tells me that Diana goes to Whittier, so the house will be very convenient for them. She can walk to school."

"Yes, indeed," Ann said vaguely, obviously lost in her own train of thought. Then, as if coming out of a reverie, she added briskly, "But you've seen George Trevelyan, Connie. He and his wife were at the Symphony Benefit when you and your parents and Tom and I went last year. Tall and dark and brooding—you know, a little like Laurence Olivier as Heathcliff, only older. And Amanda Trevelyan—what an incredible beauty *she* was! Red hair, dead-white skin, brilliant green eyes you could see a mile away, a wonderful figure she knew how to call attention to. I pointed them out to you. They were a striking couple, and I must say it was very hard to believe the gossip about them!"

Ann's comments jogged Connie's memory, and the

image of a glamorous duo sitting in a box came back to her; she had caught a glimpse of them later, during intermission, chatting with friends, and they had seemed an enchanted couple. No wonder Ann had found the stories hard to believe.

"I'm hopelessly intrigued," Connie said, amused by Ann's efforts to extract some drama from her connection, however tenuous, with the sophisticated Trevelyans. "However," she said, looking at her watch, "right now I'd better go in and see what I have to do before I meet this man of mystery. We have an appointment in Mr. Hamilton's office at two this afternoon."

"Let me know what happens, Connie, won't you?" Ann paused. "Having George Trevelyan as a neighbor would certainly liven things up around here!" Giving Connie a final hug, she turned back toward her own house, then stopped again, saying warmly, "Don't forget, call us if we can do anything, Connie. Anything at all."

"I will," Connie promised. "And thanks, Ann. It really does help to know I'm not alone."

But even as she walked up the wooden steps to the verandalike porch, even as she determined to be strong about what had to be, Connie faced once again the fact that alone was exactly what she was. An only child, an orphan, and—hardest of all to take in—irretrievably an adult now that the two people who had so lovingly seen her through her childhood were dead. In spite of all those late-night dormitory conversations about making a life for oneself, she realized she wasn't ready to be quite as grown-up or independent as all that.

Unlocking the front door, she walked into the spacious hall of the empty house that had originally been her grandparents' home. Like all those turn-of-the-century houses, it had marvelous areas of wasted space, little nooks and crannies, like the landing of the staircase with its windowseat where she had done so much reading and daydreaming as a teenager.

The sight of the hall and the staircase triggered a bittersweet memory—her father waiting at the foot of the stairs the day she was to graduate from Whittier, watching as she descended in her long white dress. His expression had been more than just proud and admiring; there was a bit of sadness in it too, and when she reached the bottom of the stairs, he had said softly, "Oh, dear, Connie, it's all gone so fast." She hadn't thought about time from his point of view until that day.

This was going to be every bit as hard as she had thought it would be, her good resolutions notwithstanding. The house was haunted with memories, and even worse than the memories was the realization that on some level she was more than half-expecting to hear the sound of her mother's quick tread, to smell her father's pipe. It was as if the house was not deserted, but a stage waiting for the actors to return—and yet she knew that they never would.

The ringing of the phone jarred her. There was something almost ghostly about it. Who knew she was there?

"Connie? It's Marjorie. I'm still over in Washington, but Mother told me you were going back to the house this morning and I thought I'd call to see how you were bearing up under Ann Bennett's sympathy."

"It's not easy," Connie replied, surprised to hear herself laugh. "She means well, but she broke down again, and more tears is the last thing I need."

"Well, I'm glad to hear you sounding more like your old self."

"Not really, Marjorie. The old self was part of the old life. What I need now is a new self and a new life."

"Then I've got just what the doctor ordered," said Marjorie eagerly. "I've landed a job with the National Arts Council and it turns out they're looking for somebody in music. Why don't you come over to Washington tomorrow and try for the job? If you get it, we can room together. It'll be like old times."

For a moment Connie was tempted. But that "old times" rang in her ears; she knew she was right about needing something new.

"And guess who I ran into?" Marjorie rattled on. "Dave Allen. He's sharing a house in Chevy Chase with five other guys. Which means we'd both have a good start on our social life. How about it?"

Connie remembered Dave Allen, and she knew the kind of men he was likely to have as friends. They were sure to be nice boys, but that was just it—they were boys and would be for some time to come.

"I don't know, Marjorie. I'll have to think about it," she said evasively, glancing at her watch. She had three hours before she was due in Ed Hamilton's office, not any too much time for what had to be done. "Look, I've got to go now, Marge. Let's talk about it when you get back, okay?"

One thing at a time, she thought, and sizing up the situation decided that she could move any things she didn't want strangers using or handling—like her mother's beloved bone china demitasse cups, her grandmother's prized Duncan Phyfe chairs, or her father's onyx desk set into the guest room and close it off. The actual emptying-out of closets and drawers could wait till the next day. From what Ed Hamilton had said, the more furnished the house was, the better. Trevelyan had evidently lost everything in the blaze and would probably want all the kitchen, pantry, and linen closets left intact, though she'd better make sure of that this afternoon. Renting the house to him certainly seemed like a good solution.

She found herself wondering what the real story about George Trevelyan was. Ann Bennett was not given to idle gossip, but she had certainly not been her usual matter-of-fact self where he was concerned. I'll ask the Hamiltons this evening, Connie decided—though if Ed Hamilton was also Mr. Trevelyan's lawyer, she supposed he wouldn't be able to say very much about his client. But he certainly hadn't suggested that there had been anything the slightest bit odd when he first mentioned the prospective tenant.

Getting a grip on herself, Connie began to tackle the job of preparing the house for the new occupants, whoever they might be. As she carefully went through the downstairs rooms, she realized that there actually wasn't much to do. To the demitasse cups, chairs, and desk set were added her grandmother's Canton plates, her mother's favorite music box, and the white Limoges porcelain cat her father had brought home on his return from a trip to France. For some inexplicable reason, her mother had *loved* that cat, and her father had kept promising her that someday they'd all go to France and she could increase the menagerie. Now that "someday" would never be . . . Connie gently set the cat down on the bureau, took a last look around, and closed the door behind her. It wasn't even twelve o'clock and she had finished.

What to do for the next two hours, she wondered, quickly washing up and running a comb through her hair. She wasn't very hungry, but supposed she ought to eat something. If she had known she would be free this early, she could have made a date to see one of her old Whittier friends, but there had been no way of knowing, and to tell the truth she still wasn't much in the mood for socializing.

Hurrying downstairs, overcome by a sudden, sharp desire to get out of the house, she decided to just drive around for a while. On the porch she paused for a moment, caught by the scent of the honeysuckle and almost overwhelmed by the memory of all the Junes of her life. Then she walked determinedly to the little Toyota Marjorie had lent her before going to Washington to job-hunt.

Well Marjorie had found her job, but as for herself, Washington was too close to what had been home. Although she had told Marjorie she would think about it, in her heart she had already decided against the idea. However, there had to be some serious thinking about what her next step should be; the demand for music majors was hardly overwhelming. New York was always a possibility, of course, but its high rents and crazy pace didn't seem all that appealing. Maybe Boston, where she already had friends settling in, would be right. One thing was sure—she didn't want to be alone in Baltimore! Even before her parents had died, she had planned to take the summer off to decide what she wanted to do, and now it seemed a better idea than ever. Oh well, I'll think about it tomorrow, Connie muttered, repeating the Scarlett O'Hara catch-line that had gotten her through four years of college crises.

Turning off Roland Avenue onto University Parkway, she slowed down to take a good look at Whittier. It was here that she and Marjorie had met, way back in first grade. At the entrance to the school, with its familiar low buildings, a couple of girls in green uniforms were standing and talking. Seeing them brought back a thousand memories: the school plays, which she had loved being in; the recitals—it was here that Connie had discovered the love of music that had led her to be a music major in college; her teachers, her girlfriends, her first boyfriends from the nearby boys' school . . .

Oddly, these memories were not at all painful. In fact, the feeling was almost comforting, giving her a sense of continuity, and on an impulse, Connie decided to spend the time before she was due at Ed Hamilton's office reacquainting herself with Baltimore and her past; maybe she'd get some clues to her future.

Heading down University Parkway, she cut through the Johns Hopkins campus. The road she was on emerged on the far side of the campus at the back end of the Baltimore Museum of Art. The sight of it brought back all the Sunday afternoons spent there with her father when she was growing up. A good amateur painter himself, he had opened her eyes to many wonders, although she hadn't always understood what he was talking about. One thing he had said did come back clearly: "Always try to keep yourself open to new experiences, Connie. In life as well as in art." Well, she would try.

For the next hour she drove around aimlessly, letting the car and her memories wander at will, until she found herself all the way downtown at the Lexington Market. The combination of hunger pangs and a miraculously available parking spot made up her mind for her. She would get something to eat from one of the market stalls. That would be much less depressing than sitting by herself in a coffee shop, her original plan.

Moving through the friendly crush of lunchtime shoppers in the market, Connie was glad she had decided to go in. You didn't have to feel lonely here even if you were alone. And everything looked and smelled so good: the mounds of cheeses, pyramids of fruit, breads of all kinds, shellfish in profusion on beds of ice, salamis hanging from hooks—delicacies from all over the world. And then her eyes fell on something that was uniquely Baltimore: the stand in front of her was selling crabcakes! She hadn't had one in a long time, and she suddenly felt a real desire for food. A few seconds later she was biting into a crabcake, delighted to find it every bit as good as she remembered—crisp and brown on the outside, succulent and moist and nicely seasoned on the inside.

As she handed the sullen counterman a ten-dollar bill and stood waiting for change, she heard someone beside her say, "I'll have one of those, too." The voice was so deep, so rich, so resonant, that Connie impulsively turned to see the face that went with it. Her first impression was that of strength: a tall, angular man in his mid-thirties, with luxuriant black hair, well-defined cheekbones, square jaw, firmly modeled lips—and clear gray eyes that met and held hers without embarrassment. An attractive man, despite his vaguely disquieting air of total self-possession, but more important, an interesting-looking one.

The counterman slapped some coins and bills down in front of her and turned to serve his other customer.

"I'm sorry, but this isn't right. I gave you a ten-dollar bill, and you've only given me change for a five."

"G'wan, lady," came the surly reply. "You're the second one to try that on me today. You gave me a five, and there's the change from a five."

Connie was about to object when the stranger beside her spoke up with quiet authority. "You're mistaken, I'm afraid. I saw the lady hand you a ten-dollar bill."

"Look, mister," began the counterman, "why don't you mind—"

With an impatient gesture, the stranger had shifted the summer jacket he carried from his right to his left arm, and Connie could see his lean but powerful body tense under the thin, white tapered shirt. He leaned slightly over the counter, his steely gray eyes blazing with a barely contained violence that was not lost on the counterman, who involuntarily stepped back.

"Well, if you say you actually saw her give me a ten . . ." the counterman said truculently, hating to give in but recognizing a will stronger than his own.

"I not only say, I insist!" The stranger's voice was still low and his tone cool, but everything about him telegraphed white-hot anger, a rage ready to erupt at the slightest provocation.

Surprised by what she felt to be a greatly exaggerated response, Connie turned to the man. "It could have been an honest error," she said, smiling her thanks for his help.

For a moment there was no reply. He raised one dark eyebrow and seemed to consider her remark dispassionately. When he finally answered, his voice was arrogant. "I think not." There was no arguing with that tone.

All the while his eyes never left hers, and there was something about that unhurried appraising stare that made her blush. Her mind was suddenly a blank, and she felt uncomfortable. Quickly picking up the bills from the counter, she nodded a final acknowledgment and moved away.

Her earlier pleasure in the sights and smells of the market was spoiled, however. Several times she caught sight of that oddly unsettling man, and each time she looked his way she found he was staring at her unabashedly.

His attention flustered her; he made no effort to approach her—if this was a pickup, it was different from any other she'd experienced—and yet he seemed ever-present! Connie had no illusions about being a great beauty, but she had had her share of masculine attention. Certainly this was not the first man to look at her with interest, even desire, but she had to admit that he was the first to look at her in a way that so disturbed her.

When, a few minutes later, she found herself outside heading for her car, she saw that the dark stranger had also come out and had just flagged a cab. Not a mean feat, Connie thought with both amusement and admiration, remembering how hard she had always found it to get a cab in Baltimore. Obviously the trick was to behave as if there could be no question about getting what you wanted.

It's funny, Connie thought as she drove away, how sometimes you notice one person in a crowd. Now that she could no longer see him, she really couldn't imagine what had so intrigued her about their . . . their what? One could hardly call it a meeting. There seemed to be no right word for what had passed between them.

On a side street near Ed Hamilton's office, Connie noticed a car pull out from the curb. It must be my lucky day, she thought, as she skillfully maneuvered the Toyota into the vacated spot. Since she still had fifteen minutes to spare, she wandered in the direction of Mt. Vernon Place, swept by memories as she walked. Up ahead was the Peabody Institute, where she had studied music after school. As she reached the Washington Monument, she stopped to survey the old houses, among the finest in the city. Many an hour had been spent sitting in this square with friends before or after her music classes. Her eyes took in the square and came to rest on Mt. Vernon Place Church, on the steps of which a bridal party had just appeared. The bride and groom looked young—they were probably just out of college, too, Connie thought. Wistfully she envied their being together. That afternoon she had staved off loneliness by grabbing something to eat at the Lexington Market, where she was surrounded by a jostling crowd. But what of the days to come? Seeing the bride and groom made her poignantly aware that there was no one special in her life, no one for whom she was the most important person in the world.

A clock struck two and she jumped up. It would be just like her to end up being late after arriving so early. Turning quickly, she saw someone rise from a bench that had been hidden from her view before. It was the man from the market, only now his expression was no longer stern and arrogant. Instead of assurance, every line of his body betrayed weariness, a weariness that Connie recognized from her own experience, and that she knew had nothing to do with physical exhaustion. With an almost visible effort at pulling himself together, he straightened his shoulders, buttoned his shirt collar, drew a tie from his pocket and deftly knotted it, then headed off in the same direction as Connie. As he walked he put his jacket on, and each of these additions was like another layer of armor. Something made her hesitant to pass him; it was almost as if she knew that he would resent having been observed with his guard down, and although she was late, Connie slowed her pace.

But to no avail. They were both walking in the same direction; and in another moment Connie noticed, with mounting excitement, that they were both going to exactly the same place—Ed Hamilton's office.

# Chapter Two

And now George Trevelyan—the "dark stranger" as Connie had previously thought of him—was sitting across from her, studying her with an enigmatic smile.

From the moment she had walked into Ed Hamilton's spacious high-ceilinged, parlor-floor office and been introduced to George Trevelyan, she had felt the magnetic pull of his personality. Ordinarily she would have been interested in seeing how Marjorie's father—she could only think of Ed Hamilton as the father of her best friend—functioned as the highly respected and busy lawyer he was. Ordinarily she would have been interested in seeing how he—or some designer, more likely—had turned what had been a residential apartment into this unusual, elegant, and yet very functional suite of offices. But ever since she had been introduced to George Trevelyan and shaken his hand, nothing had been "ordinary." That simple contact had set her every nerve a-tingle, making her more physically aware of herself than she had ever been with any of the young men she had dated in college.

The two of them were seated facing Ed Hamilton at opposite corners of his desk, an arrangement that made it possible for all of them to see and speak to one another easily, yet Connie had hardly heard a word. Her eyes had never left Trevelyan's face, nor had he broken the contact between them, though he had spoken to Ed Hamilton, had answered questions and even asked them. Connie hadn't listened to anything that had been said, was aware only of that strong, vibrant voice; she hoped that its effect on her was not obvious.

And now he had that strange smile on his face. What did it mean? What could he be thinking of to make him smile like that? Her heartbeat was so loud that she was sure she would never hear anything over the sound of it again, but just then her name was spoken and the spell was broken—though she was sure it was only because Trevelyan had wanted it that way.

"What do you think, Connie?" Ed Hamilton asked.

Connie suppressed a laugh; not only could she not tell him what she thought, she didn't even know what he had been talking about!

Trevelyan came to her rescue. "Suppose you restate that, Ed," he said with that easy assurance she already recognized as being so natural to him.

Now that Connie was no longer caught in that magnetic trap, she could feel herself blushing, to her intense annoyance. It was almost as though she had been exposed, as if George Trevelyan had taken her over—read her mind, her soul, her body, and then come to some decision.

"The point is," Ed repeated patiently, "we can draw up a year's lease starting in the fall, with an option for you, George, to buy if you, Connie, decide against keeping the house. George here, as you know, is willing to take the place furnished. As a matter of fact, it's very much to his advantage to do so, and it seems to me that it's also to yours, Connie. You won't have to decide what to do with the furniture or anything else at this point. I would say, acting for both of you as I am, that I really think this is a perfect solution for two very unusual sets of needs."

He paused and turned back to Trevelyan. "Just when is it you're planning to leave for France, George?"

Trevelyan turned his attention almost reluctantly to Ed Hamilton. Connie knew—even if the lawyer didn't —that this was the first time during the entire session that business, pure and simple, was on his mind.

"Well, Diana is due at the Lycée Voltaire in Aix-en-Provence the first week in July, so we'll probably fly over the last week in June. I have business in Paris with one of our French affiliates that'll keep me tied up over there for most of her summer school session, and I thought we could travel together for a few weeks at the end of August."

"That means you'll want the house from the first of September on. Does that sound all right, Connie?"

"Oh, that'll be plenty of time—more time than I need," she replied, as in her mind's eye the whole horrible summer stretched endlessly before her.

"I know this must be a very difficult period for you, Miss Wyatt," Trevelyan said, the intensity of his regard this time combined with a note of sympathy in his voice. "Would it be easier if I took over earlier?"

Connie was struck by the way he phrased it. The thought of his "taking over" was not unappealing. Even his unspoken but unmistakable understanding of her loss was different from everyone else's. She was sure that he understood at a level deeper than words, just as she thought she could understand how he must feel about the death of his wife.

As her eyes rested for a moment on his strong, competent hands, she noticed the unusual ring he wore:

an intricately carved moonstone in a heavy gold setting. She would have loved to get a closer look at it, but somehow couldn't see herself making this request of George Trevelyan. Not that anything in his manner had been unfriendly—far from it, she thought, remembering the sensation of total communication she had felt earlier. It had more to do, she decided, with her own unsettling curiosity about what it would be like to touch those hands—or more precisely, what it would be like to be touched by them. She was aware that in the crackling sensuality of George Trevelyan's presence she was all but gasping for air.

Willing herself not to let any hint of her thoughts appear in her voice, she said firmly, "Fall will be fine." Then, more softly, "It's kind of you to be concerned about me, when I know this must be at least as difficult a time for you."

George Trevelyan's face hardened and his eyes took on a distant look; it was as if a sheet of glass had come down between them, so that they could still see one another but all communication was sealed off. Connie wondered what she could have said wrong—and then, remembering what Ann Bennett had reported—asked herself whether she should have said anything at all.

"How's Diana coming along, George?" Ed Hamilton, once again the kind-hearted friend instead of the efficient lawyer, broke into the awkward silence. "Do you think being away from you this summer will be disturbing to her? The poor kid has had a very rough time, you know, and that's a difficult age anyway."

"She seems to be doing fine. I suspect kids are made of sterner stuff than we give them credit for, Ed. Obviously, I've been spending a lot of time with her, and I'll be running down to Aix this summer to visit her." He spoke with a curtness that made it clear that any further discussion of his private affairs would not be appreciated.

"Well, I do think getting her away from Baltimore for a while is a good idea," Ed Hamilton said, insisting on a final comment. "It might be just the thing for you, too, Connie," he added, turning to her fondly. "Not that we don't enjoy having you with us. You know you're welcome to stay as long as you want," he added quickly, afraid he might be misunderstood.

Connie smiled at him reassuringly. She knew she was welcome in the Hamilton home—in the Bennett home as well, for that matter—but somehow the knowledge didn't keep her from feeling homeless. She had no immediate answer for George Trevelyan when he turned to her and asked politely but impersonally, "What *are* your plans for the summer, Miss Wyatt?"

"I'm afraid I haven't made any yet." She hated being asked the question. It only called attention to her quandary.

"Would you two excuse me for a minute?" Ed Hamilton rose from his chair. "I want to get this agreement typed up."

"I don't know what I would have done without the Hamilton family in the last few weeks!" Connie said impulsively, turning to Trevelyan.

"Yes, it must have been very comforting to be taken into their home." His face clouded over. "Diana and I have been camping out at the Inn at Cross Keys. It's not the perfect solution, but at least it's convenient to Whittier, and Diana will be able to finish what's left of the year without too much trouble."

"She can walk to Whittier from our house—" Connie stopped short, embarrassed by the ambiguity of that "our."

"I went to Whittier myself," she added in a rush.

"And you know, I have to confess that I had some reservations about renting to strangers, but I find I like the idea of you and your daughter in the house." Was that equally ambiguous? she wondered anxiously.

If it was, Trevelyan appeared not to notice. "I'm glad you feel that way," he said briskly. Then his voice unaccountably softened. "And I promise you that we'll take very good care of your home."

"I'm sure you will," she replied, thinking to herself that he did seem the kind of man who would take good care of everything entrusted to him.

His quick, responsive smile revealed still another facet of this strange man's complex character. He seemed brighter, younger by far than the man who had looked so weary to her as she had observed him in Mt. Vernon Place. And easier, more open, less intense—though in no way less attractive—than the man who had earlier intrigued her at the Lexington Market. She had been excited by that feral, untamed quality, but she was pleased that the tension and awkwardness that it had aroused in her were gone.

It was easy to talk to this man: he was charming and intelligent, quick to pursue her conversational leads and make her feel equally charming and intelligent. She experienced a kind of elation, although they were discussing only trivial things. As they chatted, they discovered many interests in common, not the least of which, he pointed out with a smile, was a shared weakness for crabcakes. This was his first acknowledgment of their earlier meeting.

"Incidentally, I must apologize. You were probably right, and I never thanked you properly for coming to my defense."

"Of course I was right." There was an abrupt flareup of his earlier arrogance, but then he looked at her and added more simply, "I was glad I was there to do it." He paused. "I often stop at the Lexington Market since I don't enjoy eating lunch alone."

It was obviously difficult for him to make even the slightest personal comment, and, recognizing this, Connie matched his confession with her own. "That's exactly why *I* went there today."

"We seem to have more and more in common."

Before Connie could reply, Ed Hamilton burst in. "Well, I hope that wasn't too long a wait," he said as he handed them copies of the rental agreement to sign. Eager to resume her conversation with Trevelyan, Connie scribbled her signature without reading the document.

"Hey," said Ed Hamilton. "Not so fast! Don't you even want to see what you're signing?" The lawyer in him was obviously disturbed by her precipitousness in accepting the terms. Or was he responding to something he had sensed in the air? Suppressing a smile, Connie decided that it was extremely unlikely. She was behaving like a romantic schoolgirl and letting her imagination run away with her.

"No," she said firmly. "I have complete confidence." But though she was talking to Ed Hamilton, as she raised her eyes from the document they rested on George Trevelyan. At first she thought he had understood and was pleased, but she must have been wrong, because his response was merely to raise one dark eyebrow and say sardonically, "Confidence, Miss Wyatt, is what one has until it is replaced by experience. Better curb that charming innocence of yours before it gets you into trouble."

Her eyes flashed angrily. "I've had my share of experience, Mr. Trevelyan—not all of it happy—and I know that you can't live without confidence!"

Trevelyan made a visible effort to control the temper that her response had aroused, but then caught her eye and smiled ruefully. It was a peace offering, she knew, and, also smiling, she accepted it as such.

Ed Hamilton interrupted in an attempt to smooth things over. "Now, now, Connie, George has a point. You should never sign anything without reading it first." This was totally unnecessary; the storm was over long before he could usher them both to the front door.

In a move that was both natural and casual, Trevelyan took Connie's arm as they were going down the stairs. She was acutely aware of the touch of his hand on her skin, of the proximity of his lean body with its suggestion of concealed power. It was as if all her senses had suddenly been concentrated on that part of her in physical contact with George Trevelyan. His low, resonant voice sounded familiarly in her ears, sending a chill down her spine. Was it only two hours ago that she had heard that voice for the first time? It hardly seemed possible.

"Miss Wyatt . . . Connie?"

"Please . . . George," she said.

"Are you in a hurry, or do you have some time to walk with me?"

Her consent was unspoken, a mere smile, and they started to stroll toward Mt. Vernon Place. As they passed by the little strip of park that led to the monument, George Trevelyan gestured toward a bench. "Shall we sit for a few minutes first?" Connie nodded. "You know, I was early for our appointment at Ed's, so I was here for a while before."

It was on the tip of Connie's tongue to say, Yes, I saw you, but remembering how vulnerable he had looked, she decided against this. More than ever, it seemed intrusive to have seen him so unguarded.

"Sometimes things happen that really up-end your life and you don't quite take them in at the time." His voice was low, almost as if he were talking to himself. Then he added, again turning his attention to her, "But I needn't tell you what that's like, I'm sure." He shifted his position, moving his body toward hers and putting his arm along the back of the bench behind her. Connie was acutely conscious of every move he made, aware that his hand was just a fraction of an inch from her arm, his body close enough so that she had only to relax a bit to be against him. She felt rigid from the deliberate effort not to give in to that desire.

"Yes, I know what you're saying. I'm just beginning to sort things out for myself," she replied with what she hoped was a matter-of-factness that covered her inner tension. "I feel as if I've been in some kind of trance."

"Like Sleeping Beauty." George Trevelyan nodded his understanding, then added bitterly, "Only in that story the prince comes along and puts everything to rights."

Yes, Connie thought. With a kiss. And if this were a musical I would say that, and we would both burst into song and dance off into the future. She had to laugh at the notion of George Trevelyan singing and dancing a partner into the sunset, and at her laugh he looked at her with amused interest.

Seeing his quizzical expression, she said evasively, "I was just thinking that even as adults we want those stories to be true, at least we want adult versions of them."

"Fairy-tale romance," he said, suddenly sober. "Well, sometimes you think you've found yourself in one—and then the beautiful princess turns out to be a cruel enchantress." His eyes blazed with a sudden fury, but he immediately controlled himself and added, making an obvious effort to lighten the mood, "Or the handsome prince remains a frog forever."

They looked at each other, and this time both of them laughed.

"It sounds as if you don't believe in romantic love." Connie's voice was low and grave, and she kept her eyes on his as she waited for his reply.

"Not exactly." He matched her tone and answered carefully. "I'm suspicious of immediate attraction—instant love—being bowled over. Call it what you will. I'm not sure it isn't just a socially accepted form of insanity."

There didn't seem much to say to this, and Trevelyan, prodded by her silence, added, "You think I'm cynical?"

"No, not exactly."

"What, then?"

"I'm not sure." She was about to say "disappointed," but that seemed too familiar a comment to make to someone she barely knew, even if she did trust her intuitions about him. Eager to shift the drift of the conversation, she said instead, "I guess I believe in instant connections. Maybe it has to do with knowing yourself, what matters to you. Then someone comes along and everything they say, every reaction, seems right—like some kind of perfect pitch."

"It sounds as if the 'prince with perfect pitch' has already found you." It was said lightly, but a question that begged an answer was implicit.

"No, not at all," Connie replied. "Not at all."

As if he now had the information he wanted, George Trevelyan rose abruptly. "Here I've suggested a stroll and I've kept you rooted to a park bench." He looked down at her, his eyes warm and smiling. "Would you like to walk a bit?"

"Yes, fine."

As Connie stood up her heel caught in a break in the pavement, and she almost lost her balance; George immediately placed a protective arm around her shoulders to steady her and kept it there as they headed toward the center of Mt. Vernon Place.

"You know," he went on conversationally, "I've been spending so much time down at the harbor on the restoration project that it's been months since I've been in this part of town." What he said seemed deliberately bland, as if to defuse the fact that he still had his arm around her lightly. "It's one of my favorite spots in Baltimore."

"Mine, too," she said, happily aware of his touch. "It has been for years, ever since I first started coming down to the Peabody for music lessons."

"When was that?"

"Ages ago." Calculating rapidly, she added, "I was nine years old, so that must be thirteen years ago."

"Thirteen years ago," George repeated. "Thirteen years ago Diana was born." His grip on her shoulder tightened as he said slowly, "I had just become a father and you were only nine years old . . ." He seemed to notice his hand on her shoulder for the first time and turned her around to face him. Slowly his gaze traveled the length of her body, taking it in as if committing it to memory. Then deliberately he let go of her and stepped back.

Connie stood, incapable of movement, at first bemused, then oddly stirred by that last long look. It had none of the passion of their earlier encounter, when she had felt herself being absorbed, every pore of her into every pore of him, an almost physical pull of each to the other, though neither had moved. This look was almost as if he were studying her one last time, and she could see the quick play of emotions pass over his handsome face—interest, tenderness, regret, and, at the end, that final concealing curtain of detachment. There was nothing she could say, so she remained silent, standing utterly still, closing her eyes for a moment.

"Well," he said, after what seemed an eternity, "I mustn't keep you any longer. Can I get you a taxi?"

The words stabbed at her. Connie had noticed before that when people wanted to get rid of you they always said something like, "You must be busy," or "Don't let me keep you."

After a moment she managed to say coolly, "No, thank you. My car's right around the corner. Can I drop you anywhere, Mr. Trevelyan?" She hoped he would notice that "Mr. Trevelyan," but his expression remained impassive, closed off.

"No, thank you. We'll be in touch when I return from Europe," he added, with a note of finality suggesting the end of anything but a business relationship.

And then he was gone, as suddenly as he had appeared beside her at the Lexington Market.

Standing there, more alone than ever, Connie tried to remember what they had been talking about just before he removed his arm from around her. She wondered briefly if she had said or done something to offend him, but knew with a certainty she couldn't explain that that wasn't it. Perhaps, as Ann Bennett had suggested, he was just a very strange man—moody, difficult, more than a little mysterious.

Now that he was no longer there, she could be more objective about him. The sensation of feeling let down made her realize how exhilarating she had found this last hour, and how she had unconsciously been looking forward to spending the afternoon with George Trevelyan. She shook her head briefly as if to clear away all thoughts of him, all the strange excitement of the past hour. Even if she had been wrong in thinking they had made an emotional connection, she could swear that the physical attraction had been completely mutual. What had happened? "Confidence," he had said, "is what one has until it is replaced by experience." She had to admit that her experience was of no help in understanding George Trevelyan.

Forcing herself to throw off her confusion, Connie decided that before going back to the Hamiltons, she would pay a visit to the Symphony Bookshop and Coffee House, a favorite haunt of hers for years. The shop's owner often picked up interesting old music books at auctions and estate sales. She could kill an hour or so browsing through the shelves to see if anything struck her fancy.

Half an hour later, Connie came across a real find, a dusty old copy of *Plaisir d'Amour*, a collection of turn-of-the-century French songs. Flushed with success, she decided to celebrate her luck by having a cup of coffee at one of the café tables at the back of the store. Usually tables were at a premium there, but at this hour of the afternoon the café section was empty except for one person: a frizzy-haired, dumpy woman of indeterminate age in a blue and white suit that Connie recognized instantly as belonging to "Old Periwinkle," as the girls at Whittier had called their French teacher. She had been wearing that very same shapeless suit the first time Connie had ever laid eyes on her as, standing in front of the class at the beginning of the fall term, she had introduced herself with the phrase that was now a part of Whittier legend: *"Je m'appelle Pervenche Harvitte. J'ai le nom d'une fleur."* And so naturally, after they'd looked up every word they found that it meant that her first name, Pervenche, was the name of a flower—"periwinkle." She was known forever after as Old Periwinkle. Looking at her now, and seeing that she was only in her early fifties, Connie realized that she couldn't have been all that old back then. Age was a matter of perspective, she was beginning to understand.

"Mademoiselle Harvitte!" Connie exclaimed with genuine pleasure.

The frizzy head was raised, and Mademoiselle Harvitte peered myopically in Connie's direction.

"Don't you remember me, Mademoiselle? It's Connie Wyatt."

A smile of recognition lit the teacher's kindly features.

*"Mais oui,* my child, of course I do."

As Connie reached the table, Mademoiselle Harvitte took her hand in both of hers. "My poor child," she said. "We were all so sorry to hear . . ." Her voice trailed off.

"Thank you," Connie said simply, then added, "May I join you?"

"Of course, my dear, of course," Mademoiselle Harvitte said quickly, and she began to clear a chair of the unwieldy collection of badly tied parcels, books, and string shopping bags filled with odds and ends so Connie could sit down.

"Now let me see, what college did you go to? I have so many girls, you know, that I go off the tracks."

Connie had forgotten Mademoiselle's occasional linguistic lapses, but that sentence brought it all back to her, reminding her of the gales of hysterical laughter that had greeted each new "periwinklism" as it was added to the collection handed down from class to class. Well here was something that hadn't changed over the years, any more than Mademoiselle Harvitte's two suits, one for cold weather and one for warm. The one she was wearing now was spring-into-fall; on November first it would be replaced by a vintage gray flannel. Only the blouses changed—a curious collection of incongruous pastel confections revealing, Connie now understood, the essentially romantic quality of this woman whom romance had passed by.

"I ended up going to Oberlin," she said, "because the music department was so good."

"And what do you expect to do with this music when you get out?"

Connie laughed ruefully. "But I'm already out, Mademoiselle Harvitte, and the problem is that I don't know. I *do* know I'm not good enough to be a professional singer," she said honestly. "I suppose I could go on to take a master's in music education, but I don't know if I want to teach. And at this point, it's hard for me to make up my mind about anything. But what about you, Mademoiselle? Are you staying in Baltimore all summer, or will you be getting out of the heat for a while?"

Whittier, like most private schools, didn't pay very well, and Connie knew that Mademoiselle Harvitte could probably seldom afford to go anywhere. She asked about her plans partly to be polite, but also because she found that she really cared. Now that she was beginning to emerge from her state of shock, it was as if everything she had gone through was making her more aware of other people.

"This year," Mademoiselle Harvitte replied radiantly, "I am out of luck." Connie was perplexed until Mademoiselle Harvitte added, "I'm going to spend the summer in France."

"Oh, yes. You *are* in luck, aren't you?" she exclaimed enthusiastically.

Oblivious to the correction, Mademoiselle Harvitte raced on in her inimitable way to explain that Whittier had just arranged a summer exchange with the Lycée Voltaire in southern France—in Aix-en-Provence, as a matter of fact, which was very close to the town where what remained of her family lived. "Originally we were to have four teachers, but one of them just dropped out only yesterday for personal reasons." Mademoiselle Harvitte sighed and shook her head. "Twenty girls are too many for just three women to handle," but, as she explained, none of the other teachers could take the job on such short notice, and they had not yet been able to find a reliable outside replacement.

The mention of Aix had brought Connie up short, and as soon as Mademoiselle Harvitte's voice came to a breathless halt she asked if Diana Trevelyan was one of the students included in this exchange.

Not understanding the connection, and obviously surprised that Connie even knew who Diana was, Mademoiselle Harvitte looked puzzled for a moment. "Yes, of course, Diana will be with us. It is the perfect solution for the father of this unhappy child, is it not? He can play in Paris while we try to repair her a bit."

Such open criticism of George Trevelyan from Mademoiselle Harvitte, who was generally the soul of kindness, was almost shocking. Connie was about to rush to his defense until she realized that she had no reason to—and also that she was reluctant to speak of him or of their meeting, though she was interested enough in hearing *about* him.

"But what, *ma chère,* are your plans for the summer?" Mademoiselle Harvitte asked, real interest in her voice.

"People have been asking me that all day," Connie said with a touch of impatience, "but I just can't seem to make any decisions, not for the summer *or* for the fall."

"Ah, *mon enfant*, I know you have had a terrible shock, but that makes it all the more important that you make a plan. If you don't make a plan," she said emphatically, "you will find yourself doing nothing, and then your cook is goosed!"

Connie burst into peals of laughter.

Pleased to hear her laugh but bewildered as to the cause, Mademoiselle Harvitte looked at her blankly. "What have I said?"

"I don't think I can explain it," Connie answered, making a mental note to share that periwinklism with Marjorie as soon as she got back from Washington.

For a moment Connie was afraid she might have hurt Mademoiselle Harvitte's feelings, but the French teacher was already miles away, a beatific, satisfied smile on her face. "But of course," she said, "but of course. You are coming to France!"

Connie looked at her blankly.

"Yes, it is perfect," Mademoiselle Harvitte continued, pursuing her own vision. "We need a teacher, you need a change and a *situation*, a job, and you always spoke French beautifully. It is only for six weeks—a mini-plan, *n'est-ce pas?* And you can see if you like teaching. Yes?"

"But, Mademoiselle Harvitte, I can't do anything like that!"

"And why not?" Old Periwinkle challenged.

Thinking about it, Connie had to admit that there really was no reason why she couldn't go to France. She had kept up her French in college so she felt comfortable with the language. The house was arranged for; she had no commitments to anyone, no attachments to keep her here. Actually, the more she thought about it the more she felt it might be the answer for her. In fact, it was positively exciting. A new country—and one she had always wanted to visit; something new to do—she would be a teacher instead of a student; lots of new people—with a few familiar faces to keep her from feeling totally alone. And in Aix, too! There was an annual summer music festival there, she knew, and that alone was enough to make it a reasonable choice.

"How do you know they'll agree to take me on?" Suddenly the prospect of going seemed too good to be true, and she was afraid that it might be taken away from her. "Though I can speak French, I don't have any training or experience as a teacher, you know. I was never even a counselor in camp."

*"Ma chère,* to tell the truth, there will be very little teaching for you to do. Very little for any of us. The parents do not know, but mostly it is to keep an eye on the girls. Oh, don't misunderstand. We will do our best, but it is summer, after all, and it is for a taste of France, not to pass examinations, that we go."

Mademoiselle Harvitte paused reflectively for a moment. "Anyway, you need have no fears. Miss Levering is in charge of the exchange, and I remember you were always one of her favorites. We will go to Whittier *tout de suite!* You will see. There will be no problems."

All this was said with the optimism that had always been Old Periwinkle's most endearing trait, and Connie found that optimism so contagious that within a few minutes, the time it took to get Mademoiselle Harvitte assembled with her belongings, they were leaving the Symphony Bookstore and heading for Connie's car. Burdened with a good portion of Mademoiselle Harvitte's bundles, Connie thought with amusement that she would probably be toting less luggage when she actually left for Aix. The prospect of the trip brought a happy smile to her face.

If she had been totally honest with herself, she would have admitted that the most alluring aspect of that prospect was the chance it afforded of seeing George Trevelyan again before fall.

# Chapter Three

Two days in Aix, and Connie could already see there was going to be trouble. It wasn't the girls—despite her initial fears they seemed to like her, and she didn't think she'd have any difficulty teaching them or maintaining discipline—the problem was Miss Levering and Miss Hardcastle. Having been one of Miss Levering's favorite "girls" was obviously going to make it more difficult to be accepted as one of Miss Levering's staff, Connie realized.

She had proposed that the girls attend an open rehearsal of a chamber group that was to be part of the Aix Music Festival, but both Miss Levering and Miss Hardcastle had joined forces to veto the idea out of hand. Her suggestion hadn't been considered and decided against—it had simply been brushed aside as not worth discussing.

"I'm afraid, Connie, that it takes an enormous amount of musical sophistication to listen to a rehearsal and not come away with the wrong impression. And we don't want to give these girls the wrong impression, do we?"

"We certainly don't," Miss Hardcastle agreed, as if she had been asked.

"But how can seeing how something works give anyone the wrong impression?" Connie asked, truly puzzled. "Isn't that what learning is all about? Trying something, realizing it can be improved, working on it, making it better?"

But Miss Levering raced on, unheeding. "And moreover, I don't like the idea of cutting into class time for any reason. It sets a bad precedent."

"*Such* a bad precedent," Miss Hardcastle had chimed in, as if on cue.

Little Miss Echo, that's what she is, Connie thought as she looked at her with new eyes—the eyes of a colleague. Thin, nervous, fiftyish—a good history teacher, Connie remembered, but a woman who had seemed even then to be sexless, dried out. Romance had never even brushed alongside her. None of Connie's classmates could ever imagine her ever being interested in anything except her piled-high desk at Whittier. They had been wrong, Connie realized. Everyone had some kind of emotional life, and Miss Hardcastle had obviously decided that hers was to be found in being Miss Levering's satellite. A thankless job, Connie saw in a flash of insight. Miss Levering might have noticed Miss Hardcastle's absence, but her presence was, at best, taken for granted. Miss Levering did not need Miss Hardcastle.

However, there was something about Miss Levering, especially when she smiled, that suggested beneath her stylish severity the softer, prettier woman she must once have been. There had been rumors, Connie remembered, and she could now believe them, that this cold, hard, sarcastic woman had once been in love—engaged even—but something had gone wrong, and the marriage had never taken place. How bitter that must have been! But whatever sympathy she might have felt was ruined by Miss Levering's next statement. "Take my word for it, Connie. As time goes on, you will come to see that I am right."

"Absolutely!" Miss Hardcastle agreed emphatically.

Glancing at Mademoiselle Harvitte, Connie realized that Old Periwinkle wanted to be helpful, but was intimidated by Miss Levering—and rightly so: Miss Levering was in no mood to brook oppositions.

"With responsibility for twenty giggly girls, I cannot allow someone who is little more than a girl herself to make mistakes! We will consider the matter closed."

The kindly French teacher looked at Connie and shrugged helplessly. A chill had fallen over the sun-filled dining alcove of the Lycée Voltaire. The café au lait, croissants, and loaves of crusty French bread, still hot from the bakery served with country-fresh butter and homemade jam, had lost all their savor. At the first sign of any initiative she had been squelched, and the battle lines had been drawn.

As the four women rose from the breakfast table at Miss Levering's signal, Connie shot Mademoiselle Harvitte a look of gratitude. In some curious way she felt they had become allies in what was clearly going to be a divided camp. What side would Madame Alexandre— the Frenchwoman who was the administrative head of the lycée—be on? she wondered. From the little she had seen of her, Connie felt the woman would be a strong ally or a formidable enemy, but there had been no time to really get her measure, for Martine Alexandre had left the school in a great hurry early Friday evening, almost as soon as they had arrived, saying she had a seriously ill relative with whom she felt it necessary to spend the weekend.

Madame Alexandre was Miss Levering's counterpart, and should by rights have gone to Whittier with twenty French girls. Connie hadn't been told exactly why one of the other French teachers had gone in her stead, but there was something about Madame Alexandre that suggested that school was only a occupation for her and that her real life took place outside its confines, an impression enhanced by her appearance. She was a strikingly beautiful woman somewhere in her thirties, olive skinned and slender; the deceptively simple beige dress she had worn the day she had welcomed them betrayed the hand of a skilled couturier and set her spectacular figure off to advantage. Her jet-black hair was coiled elaborately on top of her head, and she moved in a cloud of what Connie recognized as Patou's Joy. In spite of the fact that she was Miss Levering's vis-à-vis, it had needed only a moment for Connie to see that they were as different as night from day.

A gentle curve in the road brought into view a sight that drove all these thoughts from Connie's mind. She was totally unprepared for the sudden vision of the Cours Mirabeau in all its summer splendor. It was breathtaking! Mademoiselle Harvitte had described it yesterday in glowing terms, insisting it was the prettiest avenue in all of France, "More charming by far than that overrated Champs Elysées in Paris"; and seeing it now for the first time, Connie found it overwhelmingly beautiful.

Pausing for a moment at the fountain near the top of the wide avenue, Connie pushed her large sunglasses onto the top of her head and enjoyed the sharp contrast between the burning sun she had just come out of and the coolness of the street roofed over and shaded by a canopy of plane trees. At the far end was another fountain. Each side of the broad avenue was different: the north side lined with cafés and shops, the south with just a few stores and what appeared to be largely residential dwellings, an unbroken row of beautiful old houses with wrought-iron balconies, many of them held up by caryatids.

Entranced by the beauty of the scene, so different from any main street or town square she was familiar with, Connie completely forgot her earlier irritation; a feeling of well-being, of exhilaration, swept over her—a sense that anything might happen. She was glad that she had accepted this position. It would have its difficulties, as had been obvious this morning, but she had always enjoyed a challenge, and she'd just have to prove to Miss Levering that she could do a good job. There was no question about it: the Hamiltons had been right in urging her to get away. Everything was so new and different that a mere five senses seemed inadequate to take it all in; she felt more alive, more in touch with herself, than she had been in a long time, perhaps more than she had ever been. Instinctively she knew that there was a new element in her life, and it wasn't the beauty of Aix.

Swinging her straw bag, feeling the breeze mold the full skirt of her simple scoop-necked violet dress around her body, she joined the promenade of strollers and turned her attention to the scene around her. From the babble of different languages, she realized that the tourist season was in full swing, an impression confirmed by the variety of license plates on parked cars, by the number of people taking photographs, and by the excited tour groups gathered around the thermal fountains that had been famous for their curative powers ever since the Romans.

Just then Old Periwinkle materialized, shepherding

four of the girls along the other side of the *cours*. While Connie watched, three of the girls suddenly darted inside a *patisserie* as if on signal, leaving the fourth standing dejectedly alongside Mademoiselle Harvitte. It was George Trevelyan's daughter, Connie saw with a stab of sympathy.

Diana was definitely the odd girl out. On the flight over Connie had tried to befriend her, only to encounter an almost impenetrable barrier—a barrier that reminded Connie only too vividly of her final exchanges with Diana's father.

But why, she wondered with exasperation, did Diana persist in pursuing Mary Leigh Stanford, Alice Williams, and Sybil Sturgess—the three most popular girls, who formed the tightest nucleus of exclusivity at Whittier? Well, Connie decided with a sigh, the unwilling outsider was always attracted to the inner circle. It was as if only there could she find the reassurance she needed.

Watching them from across the way, Connie was aware of her strong desire to make things right for this unhappy child. George Trevelyan had said that children were more resilient than people thought, but she wondered if that were really true in this case. She found herself also wondering what George Trevelyan was doing at this very moment. Her heightened sensitivity to the physical world around her brought back the memory of her meeting with him more sharply. Never would she forget what it had felt like to have him look at her, touch her; despite his apparent dismissal of her, she confessed to herself that she really wanted to see him again. Was she so different from Diana, she wondered wryly, in wanting what she couldn't get—to connect herself with someone who clearly rejected her? Well, at least she wouldn't be so obvious about it. In any case, she wouldn't be seeing George Trevelyan for quite some time.

Just then the inseparable trio emerged from the pastry shop and rejoined Mademoiselle Harvitte and Diana. The group moved off in the opposite direction, the clique intact and in the lead, Diana and Mademoiselle Harvitte bringing up the rear.

Pleased that she had been able to avoid an encounter, Connie decided to cross over and stop in one of the cafés for a cup of coffee. Again she joined the Sunday promenade of people walking home after church, shoppers stopping into the *patisseries* and *charcuteries* for cakes and ready-made treats for their Sunday dinners, young people talking excitedly in small groups, and lovers—always lovers—walking hand in hand. Oddly content, she felt a part of the crowd and at the same time apart from it. Stopping before a *charcuterie* window she was caught by the incredible array of food tantalizingly arranged to appeal to the senses: shimmering aspics that looked like abstract paintings; hams, sausages, pâtés, smoked salmon; trays of *tomates provençales;* and a myriad of salads—sliced cucumbers, cubed beets, shredded carrots, florets of cauliflower, white beans and leeks in vinaigrette. Glancing up from the display to peer inside the shop, Connie caught a glimpse of her face reflected in the plate glass, and noticed with pleasure that she looked well as if her inner mood was mirrored in her face. She felt, she realized, quite happy.

And more than ready for a coffee and something to eat! Another of those delicious croissants, she decided gluttonously. Which café would it be, she wondered. Actually, as she soon saw, it was more a question of which café *could* it be; they were all so crowded. A group of people were leaving the one called Les Deux

Garçons, so she headed for that; unfortunately, by the time she got there only one table at the rear was left. Just as she was resigning herself to take it, two people immediately in front of her miraculously got up and vacated their table. Gratefully she slipped into the rush-bottomed chair; it felt wonderful to sit down. That long, hot walk from the lycée had been more tiring than she had realized.

With his waxed mustache and heavily pommaded, carefully parted hair, the waiter who materialized at her side looked like something out of a French operetta; his dazzling white apron and the equally white napkin draped nattily over one arm contrasted sharply with his black jacket.

"Mademoiselle desires?"

"Mademoiselle" smiled inwardly. What did she desire? Life, laughter, love, everything!—but for the moment she would settle for coffee.

"Café au lait and a croissant, please."

"Désolé," said the waiter, twisting his face into a comic expression of regret. "It's been very busy this morning and the croissants are all gone."

"Well, just coffee then."

Settling comfortably in her chair, she took in the spectacle before her. Everything she had heard about European cafés was true. It was certainly comfortable sitting here, watching the passing parade, and she decided that she could easily become addicted to café sitting and crowd watching. A part of her enjoyed the feeling of being out of the hurly-burly, but there was another side too, a side that wanted to be more actively involved in life. This was the first summer that she was not just on vacation waiting to return to school, Connie thought; this was really the beginning of her adult life. She remembered the poster on Marjorie Hamilton's bedroom wall: THIS IS THE FIRST DAY OF THE REST OF YOUR LIFE. She understood that now; from here on in, it was up to her.

The sound of a pleasant, slightly accented voice roused her from her reverie: "May I join you?"

Looking up, she found herself staring into a pair of eyes whose brilliant blue was set off by a tanned face topped by a mop of curly blond hair—unbelievably blond. She had never thought a Frenchman, a Mediterranean, could be so blond. The man was so strikingly good looking that one almost didn't notice his clothes, though the well-tailored prefaded blue jeans and tapered shirt were meant to be noticed; casual looking, they had not been casually chosen.

She smiled vaguely, and was answered with a dazzling smile in return.

"As you can see," he continued, "all the tables are taken. And since you are alone . . . and I am alone . . ."

There was something indefinable in his manner that suggested he did not expect to be refused, and though Connie considered for a moment doing so just to shake him up, she decided that he was much too attractive to turn away—that he was, in fact, just what she needed to complete the pleasure of the moment. Besides which, she noted with amusement, without waiting for her to say either yes or no, he had already pulled a chair close to hers and sat down.

"*Pastis* for me, please," he said to the waiter, who had just arrived with Connie's coffee.

"What's that?" Connie asked.

"A local specialty. It tastes like melted licorice, but it's deceptively innocent. You can try a sip, if you want. I'll be here to protect you," he added, flashing a boyishly seductive smile.

Connie had seen that face somewhere, but couldn't place it. The voice was well modulated, and his English was excellent—more British than American.

There was also no denying that he was as handsome as a Greek god and took a frankly conscious pleasure in his looks. Judging by the number of heads that were turned in the direction of their table, other people seemed to confirm him in this belief. As Connie glanced around the café, she noticed that there were other young women sitting alone, and that he had evidently deliberately chosen to join her.

She should feel flattered, she supposed—and had to admit that she did!

No reason for him to know that, though, she thought, and asked him quickly, "You spoke to me in English right away. How did you know I wasn't?"

"Do you really want to know?" He raised his eyebrows.

Darn these handsome men! They were so sure of themselves!

"Yes. I wouldn't have thought it was so obvious."

"Only to the trained eye," he said self-mockingly. It was just that self-mocking quality that kept his assurance from being offensive.

"You've studied American women?"

"Whenever possible. And one thing I've noticed is that they always push their dark glasses onto the top of their heads." He paused, taking her in appreciatively. "In your case, of course, I understand. Eyes like that should never be hidden." Something about him as he smiled candidly into her face suggested that every word he said, every movement he made, was part of an elaborate game, the rules of which had been established long ago. He was serious—and yet not very, all at the same time.

Connie laughed, frankly enjoying his open flattery.

She realized it was a game, an amusing one that fit in perfectly with her present mood.

"And what's the other thing you've noticed about American women?"

"They have a certain *je ne sais quoi,* an indefinable quality lacking in even our most beautiful women." He looked at her expectantly as the waiter placed a pitcher of water and a tall glass partially filled with a yellowish liquid on their table.

"And now I'm going to introduce you to our *pastis.* Beware." He laughed. "It may be a witch's philter, and you will end up hopelessly in love with me."

"I'll take my chances."

"Spoken like a true American."

He poured some water into the glass and stirred the mixture, turning it cloudy, and offered it to her with a flourish. *"Voilà!"*

"Interesting," she said noncommittally, after taking a sip. She thought to herself that it would take some getting used to. It was too sweet to be refreshing, and it certainly couldn't be a strong drink! It didn't taste anything like hard liquor.

As if reading her mind, he said, "Don't be fooled by how sweet it seems. Like love, it is a dangerous potion for the unwary. You're right to stick to coffee, if this is breakfast—or even a second breakfast. But why no croissant?"

"Alas," she said dramatically, "they were out of them. And I'm sorry, because frankly I'm starving."

"That's easily remedied." He reached for the musette bag he had slung over the back of his chair. Digging inside, he produced a little plastic packet filled with small diamond-shaped, cream-colored cakes. "You must try a *calisson,*" he said. "Another local specialty."

"I'd love one," she said, secretly hoping it would be

more of a success than the *pastis*. "Ummmm, how wonderful! Almonds?"

"Yes," he replied. "This part of France has always been famous for its almond trees. Have you had a chance to see the countryside?"

"Not yet. But I plan to be here for a while, so I expect I will. Do you live here?"

"No, actually I'm from Paris. I'm just in Aix for the weekend, and then I'm going on to visit friends nearby."

Her eyes lit up. "Paris," she said breathlessly. "I'm afraid the only part of Paris I've seen was the airport, when I changed planes."

"Well, that's hardly adequate," he said dryly. "But I'm sure you plan to return there for a visit before going back home. By the way, where is home—New York?"

"No. Baltimore." Not that Baltimore really was home any longer, she realized.

He seemed not to have heard her answer. "New York." His face became even more animated. "I love New York. It's so alive, it's so . . . so . . ." Words failed him, and he made a dramatic, sweeping gesture. "It's the most exciting city in the world!" he declared. "Don't you think so?"

"Well, I don't know." Connie hesitated. "Sometimes it seems almost crazy. But I've only visited; I don't know what it's like to live there."

"Perhaps what you call crazy is what I love." He flashed her another brilliant smile.

Connie decided he had to be the best-looking man she'd ever seen in her life. And yet not the most attractive. Something was lacking, something indefinable. Something she had sensed in George Trevelyan.

In many ways this man was not so very different from the popular men she had known in college. They all lived in a world of easy conquests. Everything came to them effortlessly—they laughed a lot, had lots of friends, liked to have a good time—and their sensitivity seemed to stop at the outer edge of their own skin. That was it, she realized. They didn't really care about anyone else. This man, for instance, flattered her ego; George Trevelyan had stirred something deeper in her. That was why her thoughts kept returning to him almost involuntarily.

It was not that she was impervious to the Frenchman's charm, but she was not for a moment fooled by the nature of the attraction he exerted, and she wondered what his next move would be in the amusing game they were playing. It came as a surprise to her, therefore, when he suddenly glanced at the elegant watch on his sun-tanned wrist.

"Oh, *mon Dieu!* I had no idea it was so late. I was supposed to meet someone at twelve o'clock and it's practically that now. I'll have to hurry. Too bad!" he concluded. Summoning the waiter with a wave of his hand, he shoved a bill into the man's hand as he turned to Connie and hurriedly said, "I hope you will allow me. This has been fun. Thank you."

Connie watched him leave the café and saw the heads turn as he passed.

Well, she thought, that was sudden. So sudden, she noticed, that he had even left behind the little bag of *calissons*. Since in her experience men of this type were seldom disturbed at the thought that they were keeping somebody waiting, the appointment must have been one that was very important to him.

Though she was startled by his abrupt departure, she found she really didn't care. It had been a pleasant interlude, from which neither of them had expected anything more than they had gotten. They hadn't even exchanged names.

Strange, she had spent only a little more time with

George Trevelyan, and yet the effect, the impression of that meeting, was far different—far more lasting. She didn't even want to acknowledge to herself how often he was in her thoughts, how many times she had replayed that hour in Ed Hamilton's office and the strange interlude in Mt. Vernon Place, how clearly she could still feel his presence, the touch of his hand, the magnetic field that seemed to exist between them.

As she stood up to leave, Connie was greeted by a chorus of happy voices. "Miss Wyatt! Miss Wyatt! It's us! Are you going back to the school?" Sybil Sturgess, Mary Leigh Stanford, and Alice Williams—Connie found she was beginning to think of them as the unholy trio—came rushing over. Old Periwinkle trudged along behind them, but Diana was nowhere to be seen.

"Hello, girls," Connie said. "Yes, I am. I'll walk back with you. It's past noon already and we don't want to be late for lunch." She picked up the little bag of *calissons,* and then asked, "Where's Diana?"

The girls exchanged knowing glances. "Oh, drippy Diana," Mary Leigh said with disgust. "Don't worry. She'll be along."

"Do you have a minute, Connie?" Mademoiselle Harvitte asked, and at Connie's nod she turned to the students. "Why don't you three go on ahead? We'll catch up."

The girls moved off as one, obviously delighted with even this bit of freedom, and Mademoiselle Harvitte hurriedly turned to Connie. "Those wretched girls! They are so cruel. Diana wants so much to be friendly—to have friends—and they will have nothing to do with her. It's the age, that's all. It happens every year to one girl or another, but you would think they could pick on someone else. After all, she's just lost her mother. And since her father doesn't care, someone must. *We* must!"

Connie wondered once more what it was about George Trevelyan that made people react to him so strongly. Both Mademoiselle Harvitte and Ann Bennett were quite antagonistic toward him, apparently on the basis of what they saw as insufferable self-assurance. They had misread him, she was sure. What they saw as egoism, she had seen as strength.

"Is there something I can do to help?" she asked.

Yes, there was, Mademoiselle Harvitte explained. Maybe she could talk to the girls and get them to be more accepting of Diana.

Within minutes, Diana herself came running up to them. "Guess what, Miss Wyatt. My father's coming down from Paris tomorrow and he's going to take me out to dinner! I can't wait to see him!"

Her comment momentarily obscured Connie's realization that this was the first time Diana had voluntarily spoken to her. The other students had vied for her attention; only Diana had ostentatiously ignored her and rejected her overtures. It was almost as if she were afraid to get close to any adult; as if only with the other students could she hope to find what she needed. And wanting their friendship so much, she was going about it in just the wrong way, Connie thought pityingly.

"That's wonderful, Diana," Connie said smoothly. She did think it was wonderful for Diana, but her own heart, she admitted inwardly, was beating faster too at the thought of seeing George Trevelyan.

The unholy trio was waiting up ahead, Connie noted, and she decided to seize this opportunity to speak to them. "I don't think those girls should be left alone," she said, looking significantly at Mademoiselle Harvitte before hurrying off.

On the way back to the lycée, Connie skillfully led the three girls to talk about Diana Trevelyan and found she had opened up a Pandora's box. Story upon story tumbled out, each supposedly proving just how "drippy" Diana was, none very significant from an objective point of view. Among their trivial complaints, however, was one Connie couldn't dismiss.

"The worst thing about Diana," Mary Leigh pronounced solemnly, "is that I think she's a thief."

"You mean you *know* she's a thief," Alice chimed in.

"What makes you say that, Mary Leigh?" Connie asked. "That's a very serious charge, you know."

"Ever since she came back to Whittier after the fire people have been missing things. And just yesterday I saw her in my room, and later I noticed that my silver pen was gone."

Connie said firmly, "That's not really good enough evidence."

"I just know it's Diana," Mary Leigh said righteously, "and I'm going to report her to Miss Levering."

"Before you do that, Mary Leigh, will you please do me a favor? Let me talk to Diana first."

An obvious battle was going on within Mary Leigh. Finally her desire to be in Connie's good graces conquered her innate enthusiasm for making trouble.

"All right, Miss Wyatt," she allowed grudgingly. "But I don't think it's fair for her to get away with this!"

Connie was no longer listening. She was already thinking of what she could possibly say to George Trevelyan's daughter that evening, and at the same time she found herself wondering what she would say to George Trevelyan himself when she saw him again. How strange, she mused. Just an hour ago she had been sure she wouldn't be seeing him for weeks, and now he would be there the very next day.

# Chapter Four

"*Dépêchez-vous! La cuisinière n'aime pas qu'on soit en retard!*" Martine Alexandre called out from her Fiat as she passed them at the wrought-iron gate of the low stone wall surrounding the lycée. The girls looked confused and turned to Mademoiselle Harvitte, who waved after the disappearing car and said distractedly, "She's right, *mes enfants*, the cook won't like it if we are late for lunch. Run along and wash up."

With a flurry of nervous movement she shooed them forward and turned to Connie. "You too, *ma chère.* Come along with me and we can talk."

Wanting a moment to herself, Connie hesitated. "I'll be along in a minute, Mademoiselle Harvitte."

The older woman looked at her shrewdly and nodded. "All right. But you know, if I'm to go on calling you Connie, you must start calling me Pervenche. Or . . ." she paused with a mischievous gleam in her eye, "if you want, you can always go back to Old Periwinkle." And she was gone, leaving Connie speechless. To think that Mademoiselle Harvitte—Pervenche—who had always seemed so unaware of everything around her, had known about her nickname all along! It occurred to Connie that Pervenche probably wasn't as vague about the world around her as everyone thought.

Watching her scurry up the tree-lined drive to the sprawling nineteenth-century stone building, Connie resolved that she wouldn't ever again underestimate this new friend. Then, still smiling at the memory of Pervenche's moment of triumph, she cut across the lawn to the little garden she had discovered the day before. Next to the tidy vegetable patch was a luxuriant but untended bower—a spontaneous profusion of flowers, more like an English country garden than the formal French gardens she had seen in photographs. In one corner a lush clump of golden sunflowers outlined against the brilliant blue sky reminded her that this was Van Gogh country, and she could see that the shimmering sunlight, the dazzling colors of his paintings had not been exaggerated. In another corner there was a gnarled old tree, a wooden bench circling it, and tall hedges separating it from the rest of the garden. Two old wicker chairs were further evidence that someone had tried to create a private spot for reading or daydreaming.

From inside the building came the sound of the girls calling to each other as they got ready for lunch, and Connie supposed she should be doing the same, but there was something about this moment she was reluctant to give up. Last night, unable to fall asleep and filled with vague longings, she had come down and wandered in the garden in the moonlight; this morning, awake before anyone else, she had returned and seen the garden come to life as it was touched by the rising sun. Both experiences had left indelible impressions on her. But right now, in the heat of the day, she saw that the garden was at its peak, exuding a riot of color and scent. And sound, she realized, becoming aware of the background symphony of buzzing bees and droning cicadas. Her body, warmed by the hot sun, was alive to every wisp of breeze, to every sensation, as the sensuous atmosphere of the afternoon merged into the memory of another sunlit day, when she had walked around Mt. Vernon Place with George Trevelyan. That moment in the past was so present in her that when she heard a sound behind her she turned around half expecting to find him there.

"I know that I have interrupted you," Martine Alexandre said with a knowing smile, "but from the look on your face I fear I have disappointed you as well."

"Not at all," Connie said hurriedly, still confused about what was real and what imagined. "I was just thinking . . ." Her voice trailed off lamely. She could hardly tell Madame Alexandre what she had been thinking.

Noticing her confusion, Madame Alexandre added, "Oh dear, I'm afraid I have embarrassed you."

Connie longed for a clever answer, but none came to mind. Checkmate, she thought to herself. "Perhaps you're right," she admitted with a smile, thinking that Madame Alexandre probably didn't know the meaning of the word *embarrassed*. She looked as if she had come into the world assured, sophisticated, untroubled by doubts about anything. Even her hair, caught at the nape of her neck in a beautifully arranged chignon held by a single heavy gold hairpin, was evidence of a sure eye and a surer touch. Despite the severe lines of her perfectly cut white linen suit, Madame Alexandre exuded an air of sensuality, and Connie wondered briefly if there was still a Monsieur Alexandre, and, if so, where he was. In any event, this woman was certainly a far cry from any teacher she had ever seen before. In her simple violet dress, Connie felt like a schoolgirl next to her.

Madame Alexandre broke the silence that had fallen between them. "It's hard to think of you as a teacher," she said pleasantly, her green eyes appraising Connie.

"It's funny you should say so," Connie answered with a shy laugh, "because I was just thinking the same thing about you."

"Well, I suppose neither of us is exactly typical." The tone of this indicated that to be typical was a condition to be avoided at all cost. Suddenly her eyes focused on the small bag of *calissons* that Connie still clutched in one hand. "Oh, *calissons!* You've already discovered one of our local delicacies. I adore them."

"Here, have these." Connie generously offered her the entire bag. "They were an unexpected gift."

"Admirers already?" Madame Alexandre said, taking just one with a nod of thanks. "But then I'm not surprised. You're very charming—quite fresh and unspoiled."

Although it would have been hard to explain, Connie felt there was a note of condescension in this apparent compliment. A sharp burst of annoyance at the thought dissipated her previous euphoria, and she welcomed the sound of a gong from the inner recesses of the lycée. There was a noisy clatter as the girls stampeded into the dining room from all directions, and Madame Alexandre made a tiny grimace. "Oh dear," she said, "I suppose we must join the horde."

"You don't sound very enthusiastic."

"To tell the truth, I hadn't expected to be spending my afternoon here."

"Yes, we weren't looking for you till evening. Your aunt must be better."

Madame Alexandre looked blank for a moment,

then answered flatly, "Oh, yes, she's made a remarkable recovery. A few days in bed was all she needed."

They entered the building through a side door that led directly from the garden into the dining alcove reserved for the teachers. Mademoiselle Harvitte, Miss Hardcastle, and Miss Levering were already seated, and in the dining room beyond them the girls were finding their places at the long refectory table.

As if mirroring the natural hierarchy within the lycée, a place at the round table had been saved for Madame Alexandre alongside Miss Levering; Connie slid into the vacant seat beside Pervenche Harvitte.

"What an unexpected pleasure. I had not thought I would be able to join you till this evening," said Madame Alexandre, looking around the table, her eyes alert, her bright smile directed on each of them in turn.

"It was unfortunate that you had to leave so precipitously Friday evening," Miss Levering said coolly. "It made settling in unnecessarily complicated. I had some difficulty with the kitchen staff."

"Very complicated," Miss Hardcastle commented, orienting herself to the prevailing wind. "Great difficulty."

"I'm sorry, but it really couldn't be helped. *Ma tante* was quite ill, and we here in France have a very strong sense of family."

Miss Levering was momentarily silenced. Connie was impressed by the skill with which the Frenchwoman had turned criticism of herself into a putdown of her American counterpart. It was another version of the technique she had used on Connie in the garden, when she had simultaneously complimented and dismissed her.

What could have become an awkward situation was saved by the arrival of the first course. The platter was automatically placed directly in front of Madame

Alexandre—the kitchen staff had no confusion as to who was in charge—who helped herself and passed the dish on to Miss Levering, saying, "Do have some *salade russe*," making it sound like a peace offering.

Miss Levering nodded her acceptance of both food and truce, and when Miss Hardcastle, on her other side, peered at the platter in some bewilderment and said, "Why, Cynthia, this looks just like carrots and peas in mayonnaise to me!" Cynthia Levering glared at her witheringly, causing poor Jane Hardcastle quite visibly to shrink into herself.

A burst of laughter from the other room drew Connie's attention away from her own table, and she looked around her with pleasure. The dining alcove and main dining room, separated by a low arch, were united by red tile floors that were wonderfully cool underfoot. The shutters at the windows were partially closed against the heat of the afternoon, but brilliant shafts of light came through the louvers, casting alternating bands of sun and shadow on the whitewashed walls. Against the far wall was a cypress sideboard on which were displayed large ceramic platters, their brilliant colors visible across the room.

"I see you are admiring those platters, Connie." Pervenche Harvitte's use of her name brought Connie back to her immediate surroundings. "I was just telling the others that they are typical of the work in this region."

Madame Alexandre, who had obviously heard more on the topic than she cared to and could barely disguise her boredom, reached for the carafe of red wine and refilled her glass.

Even the ebullient Pervenche Harvitte finally fell into a discouraged silence, but once more food came to the rescue. Heartened by her second glass of wine, Madame Alexandre resumed her role as hostess.

"Since you seem to be interested in local specialties, I'm sure you'll enjoy this *pissaladière*." Indeed the onion tart topped with anchovies and black olives was a success, not only as a dish but as a springboard to the neutral topic of food. The exchange of culinary likes and dislikes got them through the meal without any further difficulty.

In fact, the atmosphere around the table had relaxed considerably, and as the strong, chicory-flavored coffee was being served Miss Levering turned to Connie and ventured a change of subject.

"Since I understand that George Trevelyan will be renting your house this fall, Connie, you might be interested to know that he plans to come down tomorrow."

Connie immediately felt the tension his name always created in her, but answered calmly, "Yes, so Diana told me. She's very excited about it."

Miss Levering sailed on. "He plans to take his daughter out to dinner, and though as you know I don't really approve of breaks in the school routine, under the circumstances I had no choice but to agree."

This prospective "break in school routine" did not seem to disturb Madame Alexandre. On the contrary. "How does this child's father happen to be in France?" she asked with the first real interest she had shown.

Before Miss Levering could answer, Connie volunteered, "He's in Paris on business."

Miss Levering was not used to having the words taken from her mouth. She looked put out. "He's a very wealthy businessman from an old Baltimore family," she said, retrieving the conversational lead and turning her attention exclusively to Madame Alexandre. "I'm sure he took advantage of a business trip so that he could be close to his daughter after that unfortunate affair."

"Ah? An affair of the heart?" Madame Alexandre questioned.

"An affair of heartlessness, if you ask me," Mademoiselle Harvitte said vehemently.

"I don't believe anyone did ask you, Pervenche. You know I don't approve of gossip. Nothing is ever gained by it."

Having expressed her displeasure, Miss Levering turned again to Madame Alexandre, as if sure of her support. She looked surprised to hear the Frenchwoman say, "Perhaps not, but it's always amusing."

"In this case, there was nothing amusing," Miss Levering retorted. "The poor man's wife died in a fire that destroyed their home. That was dreadful enough, but unfortunately it occasioned a lot of gossip—simply because he's rich and prominent."

"Rich," Madame Alexandre murmured. "Now I suppose you will tell me he is good looking as well." She was only half joking.

"Not particularly. At least, I never found him so," Miss Levering said repressively.

Intrigued, Madame Alexandre directed her next question to Connie. "And you, Connie? I'd be curious to know your opinion of him."

"Well, I don't really know anything about the man. But from my brief meeting with him, I'd say he seemed perfectly pleasant."

There, she thought, proud of herself for having found such a bland statement to cover the wide sweep of emotions he had evoked in her. But even as she was congratulating herself on having avoided any comment about his attractiveness, Madame Alexandre returned to the attack.

"*Pleasant* hardly seems the right word for someone others describe as 'heartless.' Besides, what I really want to know is if you found him attractive. I would tend to trust *your* opinion about that."

She wasn't being very subtle, Connie thought. The implication was clear—Martine Alexandre wasn't interested in what any of the others had to say about George Trevelyan as a man, because she didn't see them as real women.

"I found him very attractive," she answered firmly.

All heads were now turned toward Connie. Suddenly uncomfortable, she added lamely, "And something about him inspired me with enough confidence to feel quite comfortable about renting my house to him on such short acquaintance."

The difference in tone did not escape Madame Alexandre, who said with a little laugh that failed to reach her watchful green eyes, "There's a contradiction there somewhere. An attractive man who inspires confidence is *never* to be trusted."

Their shared interest in George Trevelyan seemed to exclude the others, who were now folding their napkins and preparing to leave the table. Connie was torn between a desire to talk to this sophisticated woman about her one strange meeting with George Trevelyan and a feeling that she couldn't discuss it with anyone, least of all Martine Alexandre.

Meanwhile, ever one to have the last word, Miss Levering had paused at Connie's chair. "I'd like to speak to you for a moment."

"In that case," Madame Alexandre said smoothly, "we must continue our conversation some other time," and she glided from the dining room, leaving Connie and Miss Levering alone.

It took a moment for Connie to come back to the reality of school, and she wondered what Miss Levering wanted.

"I'm sure you realize, Connie, that the academic

load this summer is hardly a heavy one. Classes are only in the morning, and though there are some scheduled activities in the afternoon, the girls will still have much too much free time. I'd like you to think about putting together a special end-of-term program, an entertainment of some kind for our last evening here. Perhaps some scenes from a play or a musical recital—something *all* the girls can participate in, and the rehearsals can serve to keep them occupied for part of the late afternoon and evening. Think about it, will you?" She moved off without waiting for an answer, and Connie realized that it was not a request, but an assignment. "Think about it" meant "Do it."

Well, she didn't mind, but it was obvious that the real reason for bringing the topic up at just that moment had been to break into her conversation with Madame Alexandre and get everyone off the subject of George Trevelyan.

However, it was as if George Trevelyan did not want to be ignored or excluded from Connie's thoughts, for in passing through the main hall on the way to her room, she heard Mademoiselle Harvitte call to one of the girls, "Tell Diana there's a phone call from her father."

Hoping that Trevelyan was calling to say that he might be arriving earlier than scheduled, Connie resolved to speak to Diana as soon as she got off the phone. She realized that Diana would not be too receptive to her overtures after Connie had apparently deserted her for the other girls earlier that day, yet something had to be done before Mary Leigh spoke to Miss Levering.

As Connie reached her room, Mademoiselle Harvitte waylaid her. "May I come in for a moment?"

"Of course, Pervenche. What's wrong?"

The door had scarcely closed behind them before

Mademoiselle Harvitte burst out angrily, "After all these years, I still haven't gotten used to the way Cynthia Levering treats me. I am not a gossip and I am not a fool. It's not as if anything I said about George Trevelyan wasn't so—and I didn't say anything anyway."

"It's not as if anybody has ever said anything! I know he lost his wife in a fire. That's terrible, but I don't understand why people would gossip about that. What's he supposed to have done?"

"Ah, Connie, I can see that the man fascinates you, *n'est-ce pas?* No, no, don't bother answering that. I know without your telling me. Anyway, you're right. There is no mystery. It was just that when the firemen arrived, he was standing on the lawn with Diana and seemed unaware that his wife was inside the house. Later they found the poor thing in what had been the downstairs study, and nobody could understand why he had made no attempt to save the woman he had seemed so in love with."

Connie was silent. This was pretty much what Ann Bennett had said. She couldn't deny that there was something mysterious about George Trevelyan, every atom of her being had felt that from the first sight and sound of him, but that he would have let his wife—or anybody—die without attempting a rescue? Never! He was too physically alive, his reflexes too quick and assured, to just stand there idly—and much too proud as well. He would never leave himself open to the charge of cowardice. No, there was another explanation.

Connie was still preoccupied by these thoughts as she knocked on the door of Diana's room a few minutes later. Pervenche Harvitte's description of the burning house, of Trevelyan standing on the lawn with his daughter, was etched on her mind.

Her knocking brought no response, but through the door Connie could hear the sound of muffled sobs. "Diana? Diana, it's Miss Wyatt. May I come in?"

The only reply was an increase in the volume of the sobs.

Connie hesitated; she didn't know what to do. Diana had a right to her privacy—even to her unhappiness—but Connie had to speak to her.

Opening the door, she found the girl lying huddled on the bed, weeping uncontrollably.

"What is it, Diana? Is it something the other girls have said or done?"

"He doesn't care about me, any more than she did!"

"Who doesn't care about you?" Connie asked, knowing beforehand, with a sinking feeling, what the answer would be.

Rearing up suddenly in the bed, Diana turned to her. "My father!" she screamed, her face distorted by anguish. Tears streamed down her cheeks, and she gasped for breath between wracking sobs.

Connie held her for a few moments, waiting for the storm to subside. Then she reached for a tissue from the box she had noticed on the bedside table and found herself staring into the saturnine face of George Trevelyan. Picking up the small silver-framed photo, she studied it intently. What *was* the truth about this man? And why, she asked herself, did she care so much?

Another sob, softer and stifled this time, reminded her that she was not alone. She quickly replaced the photo and resolutely turned her attention back to Diana.

"Why did you say that your father doesn't care about you? I'm sure he cares a great deal."

"If he cared about me, he wouldn't break his promise."

"What promise?" Connie asked with a sudden premonition.

"He said he'd come down to Aix and have dinner with me tomorrow, and now he just phoned to say he was too busy and couldn't make it."

"Oh, Diana. I'm sorry. I know how you must feel." She did, too, she realized, aware of a real kinship with the unhappy child. Until this very moment, she had not known how much she herself had been looking forward to seeing George Trevelyan. "You must be terribly disappointed, but I'm sure that he'll be here as soon as he can." And then, as if determining to make sure he did, she added, "Would you like me to speak to him, Diana?"

The ray of hope brightening Diana's face made her look totally different. "Oh, yes!" she said eagerly. "Would you really, Miss Wyatt? Maybe he'll listen to you."

Connie doubted that George Trevelyan, having once made up his mind, could be swayed by anyone, least of all by her, but she would certainly try. He should learn not to raise hopes and then dash them so frivolously. "I'll tell you what—give me his phone number in Paris, and I'll see what I can do."

It was only as she was halfway down the stairs that Connie realized she hadn't said one word about Mary Leigh's charges—after all, it had hardly been the appropriate moment for such a discussion. In any case, it might be better to deal with that problem when George Trevelyan was there. Assuming he would respond to her request.

She found that her excitement at phoning George Trevelyan was mixed with a nervous anticipation bordering on fear. Remembering their final exchange in Baltimore, she realized she ran the risk of being snubbed for interfering in matters that did not concern her. Well, she would just have to chance it. Nothing ventured, nothing gained. And the stakes were high.

As Connie entered the school office, Martine Alexandre was just hanging up the phone, her usual urbanity marred by a look of extreme irritation.

"Oh, these men! They never turn up when they say they will, and they've always got excuses." She looked at Connie.

"I couldn't agree more," Connie said. "Diana Trevelyan is upstairs in a state because her father has broken his promise to come down and see her tomorrow. I said I'd call him and ask him to change his mind."

"I suspect you're wasting your time. A wealthy, attractive man who finds himself in Paris surely has better things to do than run to the provinces to spend an evening with a weepy child," Martine Alexandre said almost without thinking. Then after a pause: "But on the other hand, I daresay there's no harm in trying. I admit I'm curious to see this attractive man who inspires confidence. Meanwhile I must try to calm the cook. Miss Levering's dinner suggestions have infuriated her, and she's threatening to leave."

Left alone, Connie dialed George Trevelyan's hotel. Much to her annoyance, her heart was pounding like a teenager's. It was absurd, she told herself. He would undoubtedly be out, and she began marshaling her French in order to leave a message with the desk clerk.

The sound of George Trevelyan's voice took her totally by surprise.

"Oh! Mr. Trevelyan? It's Connie Wyatt. Do you remember me?"

It was his turn to be startled. "Connie! Of course I do. What's wrong? Are you calling from Baltimore?"

"No. I'm calling from Aix."

"Aix?"

72

"Yes. I'm with the Whittier group. And there *is* something wrong."

"Diana?" His voice was tight with tension, and she heard a sharp intake of breath.

"No, no, she's all right." Connie hurried to reassure him. "Well, she's not exactly all right. That's why I'm calling you. She's very upset that you're not coming down tomorrow."

After a long pause George Trevelyan answered. "Well, something important has come up, but primarily I felt it would be better to let her settle in before I came down."

"You're probably right, but you should have thought about that before you promised! She was really looking forward to seeing you, and she's taking the disappointment very much to heart. Isn't there any way that you can rearrange your plans? I know it would make a world of difference to her—and besides, I have something important to discuss with you."

"That's quite a speech," he drawled.

"I know, I have no right to tell you what to do. But Diana—"

"Yes, of course," he interrupted impatiently. "I understand, and it's quite all right." His tone changed. "How strange to hear from you, Connie. I had no idea you were going to be there this summer."

She couldn't tell whether he was pleased or displeased, and now that she had spoken up for Diana, Connie's courage deserted her. She wished he would hang up before she said something foolish. "Well, I didn't know it myself when we met. It was all very last-minute."

"The best things usually are," he said with a short laugh. "It's always dangerous to plan ahead. You know, I've often thought of our meeting," he continued ambiguously.

Connie waited in vain for him to explain. She too had thought of their meeting, more often than she would admit. But she had been confused by it—by the swing from exhilaration at being, for the first time, in almost perfect communication with someone to the plummeting letdown of being left emotionally stranded by them. A wave of panic now washed over her as she tried to figure out what aspect of that afternoon kept returning to his mind. Had she said or done something terribly foolish?

"I shouldn't have thought that with the loveliest city in the world outside your door you'd have much time for that kind of thinking." She hedged, feeling somewhat stupid.

From the receiver pressed against her ear came a short, harsh laugh. "The loveliest city in the world is exactly where one does 'that kind of thinking.' Or do you see me—" his voice was interested "—going into some Left Bank disco and boogying the night away?"

She laughed at the vision, and felt her tension evaporate. "That *was* a silly thing for me to say." And then she involuntarily added, "After all, there you are all by yourself tonight."

"What makes you think I'm by myself?" he asked, lazily amused.

She gasped. "Oh, I'm so sorry! You should have said something. I . . ."

"'*Should* have said something,' Connie? That's rather demanding, isn't it?"

"That's not fair!" Her face flamed with embarrassment and anger.

"My, my—what a touching, childlike faith you have, Connie. Do you find the world particularly fair? It seems to me that we had a discussion about a similar delusion concerning 'confidence.' Do you remember what I told you then, Connie?"

The arrogance of the man was beyond belief, but even as she wildly searched her mind for a scathing answer his mood changed, and she heard that warm, rich, seductive laugh. "You may be naïve, Connie, but it's very charming. I'm quite alone. And you have made my evening considerably more entertaining with this call. I thought all I had to look forward to was a cool drink and some colder financial statements."

"But instead," she replied, still tense, "you're indulging in long-distance sparring."

"Sparring long distance may be safer—but not nearly as satisfying—as perhaps I can demonstrate the next time we meet. Connie?"

"Yes?"

"What perfume were you wearing that day?"

"Perfume?" She was puzzled, since it was something she rarely used. Awkwardly she replied, "I don't know, unless it was that classic American scent, soap and water."

He laughed again, this time as frankly and candidly as a boy. It was, she decided, a very attractive sound, although there was something about it that suggested that George Trevelyan hadn't had much practice of late.

"Connie, Connie, I said before that I'd been thinking about our meeting. I've also been thinking about the quite unsatisfactory way it ended. I'm—"

There was no way Connie would discuss this on the phone! She interrupted hastily and said in a businesslike tone, "Then I can tell Diana you'll be coming down tomorrow as planned?" Waiting for his reply, she knew she was asking for herself as much as for Diana.

"All right, Connie. We'll talk about it when I see you. And yes, of course, I'll come. You can expect me on the three o'clock plane."

"Good. I'm sure Diana will be pleased."

"Only Diana?"

His imperturbable self-confidence was almost visible. She could imagine his dark eyebrows raised quizzically, his sensual lips curled in a knowing smile.

"Well, of course, I . . . we . . . all of us . . ." Her voice trailed off.

"Dare I give your charming confusion a flattering interpretation?"

"You can give it any interpretation you darn well please!" she spluttered angrily.

He laughed again, but differently, and his next words once more caught her off guard. "Connie, I want you to know that I'm glad you're as close as Aix."

It was the simple sincerity of these words that she chose to remember. They sang in her head—and in her heart—for the rest of the evening and for most of the night. They made up for much else in that puzzling, infuriating conversation.

# Chapter Five

"Ninety-eight, ninety-nine, one hundred!" Connie counted under her breath, then put the brush down and surveyed the results in her dressing-table mirror. The walk she had taken the day before had added a faint tan to her creamy skin; her luxuriant chestnut hair waved softly around her glowing face. She smiled at the reflected image, pleased at seeing someone again in love with life.

She rose and walked across the room to the French windows overlooking "her" garden and pushed them open, wincing momentarily as the bottoms scraped across the floor. The scent of thyme and rosemary, of roses and bougainvillea, permeated the early morning air, and she breathed in the earth smells so similar to, and yet so subtly different from, those of home.

It was going to be a wonderful day. All her previous doubts had vanished, and, although she could not say exactly why, she felt confident, optimistic, though by rights she should be feeling apprehensive. After all, not only was George Trevelyan reentering her life, but this was going to be her first day in the classroom. She knew the girls liked her as a person, but they hadn't yet experienced her as a teacher, and that might make a difference. A classroom situation was one that called for discipline, and she hoped they realized she was serious about this music course.

An insane thought suddenly crossed her mind: What would happen if she asked them to do something, and they flatly refused? Suppose that unholy trio, for instance, egged each other on to the point where she'd have to exert her authority. How would she do that?

The thought gave her pause for a moment, but she didn't really believe it would happen. After all, she knew her subject, she liked most of the students, and she was sure she could handle any normal discipline problems. As a matter of fact, she was so happy to be here in Aix that right now she felt she could handle anything, even Miss Levering and Miss Hardcastle. A sudden stab of apprehension went through her. Would she be able to handle George Trevelyan? Automatically she glanced at her watch and sighed. It would be a long day—but luckily a full one.

Wheeling back into the room, she caught a glimpse of herself in the full-length armoire mirror and stopped short, aghast at what she saw: the shell-pink full-skirted, boat-necked dress with its close-fitting bodice accentuated her firm young breasts, and the low neck exposed an almost embarrassing expanse of flesh. She couldn't believe she had chosen to wear this dress— perfect for some romantic candlelit supper—on her first day of work! The image in the mirror, which had smiled back at her only a few minutes before, now frowned disapprovingly as she remembered Miss Levering referring to her as "little more than a girl."

With horror she visualized her arrival at the breakfast table and the response of the four older women. Miss Levering would have seen the dress as proof of professional naïveté, and so, of course, would Miss Hardcastle; Pervenche would have been startled, but kind; and Martine Alexandre—who wouldn't have worn a dress like that under any circumstances!—would have found it amusing. *That* thought was enough to make Connie remove the dress as quickly as she could and toss it on the bed, still confused about how she could have made such a blunder. Then she remembered waking up, lying in bed half asleep, creating fantasy meetings with George Trevelyan. He would come upon her as she was reading in that little nook she had spotted in the garden. Or she would be waiting for him at the wrought-iron gate as his car approached. Or best of all she would be at the airport to surprise him, to meet him away from prying eyes. And in each of these scenarios she was wearing that shell-pink dress, and George Trevelyan would tell her she looked beautiful.

How silly, she thought, laughing. She'd better pay more attention to her work than she had to her outfit, or she'd deserve not to be taken seriously! Besides, he wouldn't even be here for seven hours. His words came back to her, though they had never been far away: "I'm glad you're as close as Aix." It wasn't much to build a fantasy on, but coming from a man like George Trevelyan it had to mean something. Unlike the Frenchman in the café, he was not given to playing courtly games. She knew instinctively that if he ever gave his heart, it would not be done lightly. And she couldn't deny that even after only their one meeting, what George Trevelyan did with his heart was important to her.

Pulling herself back to reality, she decided the blue denim skirt and the light blue LaCoste shirt would be a much better outfit and quickly slipped into them. Time to worry about George Trevelyan after lunch. Meanwhile she'd better get her mind onto what she would be doing with the girls that morning.

As class let out, Connie decided immodestly that her approach to a discussion about the troubadours and their songs of courtly love had been a stroke of genius. The girls had been intrigued with her comparison of the twelfth- and thirteenth-century poet-musicians and such comtemporary balladeers as Bob Dylan and Paul Simon. They'd even asked her to check the festival schedule to see if there would be any programs of that kind of music.

"That was wonderful, Miss Wyatt," Mary Leigh said excitedly as a group headed toward the dining room. "I took notes on everything you said!" As if to prove it, she held up a notebook, a silver pen clipped to its cover.

"Why, Mary Leigh," Connie asked with surprise, "isn't that the silver pen you told me you were missing?"

Mary Leigh's face turned scarlet. "Well, yes. I . . ." She hesitated, then went on in a rush. "I *did* think it was stolen because I couldn't find it anywhere, but then this morning, when I had to move my bed . . ."

Connie, more relieved than she cared to show, decided not to let her off the hook so easily. "So you made a charge against an innocent person a little too quickly, didn't you?"

"Yes, I guess so," Mary Leigh admitted grudgingly. She paused. "I asked Diana to sit with us in the dining room."

This was as much of a concession as Diana's accusers were likely to make, Connie realized, and she decided it would be best to let the matter drop.

It was at lunch that Connie's early morning fantasies about encountering George Trevelyan were completely dashed. During a pause in the general conversation, Madame Alexandre casually mentioned that she planned to drive to the airport and meet his plane.

Obviously taken aback by the matter-of-fact way in which the announcement was made, Miss Levering, after having searched her mind, could find no reason to object—though it was clear that she did.

"Why yes," she said slowly, "since you have a car, I suppose that makes sense." Then, fearing this sounded too ungracious, she added quickly, "Actually, it's very thoughtful of you to offer. Mr. Trevelyan is not part of your responsibility, you know, and I had assumed, of course, that he would take a taxi."

"This is something I do routinely when parents of our regular students visit us. It gives me an opportunity to get to know them."

She turned her dazzling smile on Miss Levering, then glanced around the table, her eyes finally coming to rest on Connie. Something in that glance made Connie feel that Martine Alexandre had been able to read her innermost thoughts, and even knew about the little twinge of—of what? jealousy?—that was gnawing at her.

"I must get a description of him from you, Connie, so I can recognize him when he gets off the plane." Her green eyes sparkled maliciously.

"It might be safer for you to have him paged," Connie replied, coolly avoiding the trap. "I doubt that he expects to be met."

With inner amusement, she discarded the last shreds of her airport fantasy, realizing she would have had to get there on foot! And her fantasy of meeting him as he drove up to the gate had not included Martine Alexandre in the driver's seat. That left the garden, and she decided wryly that she probably wouldn't need to change into the shell-pink dress just yet.

As they were leaving the dining room, Pervenche Harvitte turned to Connie with conspiratorial glee and said, "Cynthia Levering and Martine Alexandre are very well matched, I think. And Martine Alexandre and George Trevelyan—*that* combination has interesting possibilities, *non?*"

"What makes you say so?" Connie asked noncommittally.

"Well, he'll be a diversion for Martine, who's obviously bored with us, and he'll probably find her very attractive, very . . . *excessive.*"

Connie, who had been listening to her attentively, supplied the correct word almost automatically. *"Accessible."*

"Yes, of course. Accessible. And their age is right too."

"I don't see what age has got to do with it!" Connie said with involuntary sharpness, checking herself only as she became aware of Pervenche's interested look.

"Summer and winter, June and November, do not mix . . ." Her voice trailed off innocently, but her quick glance at Connie was a shrewd one.

Connie had not thought about the age difference between George Trevelyan and herself before, but it seemed to be on Pervenche's mind—and perhaps it had been in George Trevelyan's mind as well, that day on Mt. Vernon Place. She frowned, remembering his sudden shift in attitude on discovering he had become a father when she herself was only a child of nine. What she'd seen as just a simple statement of fact had obviously been much more significant to him. She had not thought of him as an "older man," but if he saw her as a young girl, there was absolutely nothing she could do about it.

"You may be right, as a general principle," she finally replied.

The qualification was not lost on Pervenche.

"Well," Connie said, her tone falsely brisk, "I'd better get ready for tomorrow's class. And by the way, Pervenche, I'm going to need your advice on the entertainment Miss Levering wants me to put together." Rapidly she explained the assignment that had been given her.

"Cynthia Levering can't bear to think of anyone being idle for a moment, can she?" Pervenche said with amusement. "Well, actually it's not a bad idea—not for the girls and not for you. Let me think." Running her fingers through her frowsy hair, she stood at the foot of the stairs and seemed to go into a trance. "Ah! I have it! For the music, why don't you use that *Plaisir d'Amour* collection, and for the play—Musset, of course! That kind of romantic melancholy always appeals to girls this age. Let me get you my copy of *On ne Badine pas avec l'Amour*. That's a good one to start with."

*"No Trifling with Love,"* Connie thought, automatically translating the title. Wouldn't it be wonderful if Pervenche was right, and there would be a few scenes in it that she could use.

Half an hour later Connie was in her room, totally caught up in Pervenche's well-thumbed copy of the play. She had meant to just glance through it, but she found herself captured by the story of a cynical older man who tragically toys with the affections of an unsophisticated young girl. Somehow it seemed much more interesting now than it had when she had read it in college.

It was three-thirty when she finished the play, and with a shock she suddenly realized that George Trevelyan could arrive at any moment. She decided against going downstairs. That would seem too eager. It would be better to remain in her room until she heard the car come up the drive. And she certainly wouldn't change her clothes; but there would be no harm in putting on some makeup.

By four o'clock she decided it was silly not to spend the time preparing for the next day's classes; after all, that's what she had planned to do originally. But by four-thirty she gave up. Her attention was so focused on listening for the sound of Martine Alexandre's Fiat that she was unable to concentrate on anything else.

What had happened? Could he have missed the plane? Or decided not to come after all? But in that case, why hadn't Martine come back? Perhaps there's been a crash, she thought with a stab of fear. What if he were hurt or—she forced herself to think the word—dead? To her astonishment, she found that the thought of a world without George Trevelyan was intolerable.

She was pacing nervously up and down her room, when the sound of a merrily honking horn drew her to the window, and she saw George Trevelyan helping Martine Alexandre out of the car with a gallant gesture. Far from being dead, he seemed vibrantly alive, making a mockery of her anxiety. Martine said something to him, and the sound of their laughter floated up to Connie's room. Almost two hours had passed since George Trevelyan's plane had landed. Where had they been? Well wherever it was, Connie thought bitterly, they had obviously lost no time in getting to know each other and were doing famously now.

This was a far different George Trevelyan from the one she had met in Baltimore. He seemed spontaneous and carefree, two qualities she had not observed in him, and even his clothes were different, more casual; the well-tailored chinos, the white short-sleeved knit shirt open at the neck, emphasized his tall, lean body, his broad shoulders, his strong arms. With her, she remembered, he had been alternately intense and circumspect, abstracted and totally concentrated on her. He had been like a tightly coiled spring, his control barely concealing the sense of leashed passions. Connie had been attracted by his silences, by his brooding quality, but this almost boyish exuberance also had its seductive charm. Had his brief stay in Paris done this to him, or was it the effect of Martine Alexandre, looking as unruffled and poised as ever in her simple black linen dress? They made a handsome pair, Connie admitted reluctantly.

Just then, in response to something Martine had said to him, he threw back his head and laughed explosively. As he did so he caught sight of Connie, and, after a momentary pause, waved.

She'd been unable to decide if she should go down at all, but now that he had seen her, she felt it would be too pointed not to. She would *not* let him see how she felt, she vowed.

On her way downstairs, Connie could hear Diana's excited cries. "Daddy! Where have you been? I've been waiting for you for hours! I thought you'd never get here!"

As Connie approached, she heard George Trevelyan say, "I'm sorry, Diana, but Madame Alexandre was kind enough to stop at the hotel so I could register and leave my luggage."

Miss Levering, who had arrived on the scene in time to hear this explanation, said pointedly, "I trust there was no difficulty?" Her tone indicated that there would have had to be an incredible difficulty to account for the lapse of time. "You had us all worried."

"Perhaps it was thoughtless of me," George Trevelyan admitted easily, "but the cafés on the Cours Mirabeau were so appealing that Madame Alexandre and I stopped for a glass of wine."

Miss Levering turned disapprovingly to Madame

Alexandre. "I would have thought you'd realize how eager Diana was to see her father."

Before Madame Alexandre could answer, George Trevelyan intervened. "I'm afraid it was all my fault. And in any event, I'm here now." He smiled down warmly at a radiant Diana.

Connie had followed the exchange with interest, relieved that all her unspoken questions had been raised by others. The answers, however, were not totally satisfactory. No answer, she had to admit, would have satisfied her. In some strange way she felt that the two hours he had spent with Martine Alexandre should have been hers.

Aware that she stood apart from the group and sensing her aloofness, George Trevelyan moved impulsively toward Connie, but his evident pleasure at seeing her was deflected as she stiffly extended her hand and said formally, "How nice to see you again."

Whatever he had been about to say was effectively squelched by the coolness of her greeting, and his own manner immediately mirrored hers. "It's nice to see you, too. You're looking well."

"Come on, Dad. I want you to see my room," Diana interjected.

Far from being irritated by the interruption, George Trevelyan seemed to welcome it. Connie, miserable at having created such an awkward situation, stood there waiting for him to understand and extricate them both with a word or a look, but he merely continued in the same impersonal tone, "I'm afraid you'll have to excuse me. Would it be possible for us to talk tomorrow morning? Madame Alexandre has offered to take us back into town so I can arrange to rent a car, and then Diana and I will be going out to dinner after that."

"Tomorrow morning will be fine. I don't have a class till eleven o'clock."

"Good. I'll be here immediately after breakfast."

"Dad, come on!" Diana again exclaimed impatiently.

George Trevelyan smiled at them all, and he and his daughter disappeared into the house.

"Ah, whatever happened to that wonderful old tradition of children being seen but not heard," Madame Alexandre said with a mock sigh.

"That was a tradition preserved by selfish adults," Miss Levering replied coldly.

Madame Alexandre seemed to be considering a sharp retort, but ended by merely shrugging her shoulders. "Before I drive Mr. Trevelyan and Diana into town, I'd better check with the cook to see if there are any problems, since I won't be here for dinner tonight."

"Again, Madame Alexandre?" Miss Levering inquired critically.

"Yes, again, Miss Levering." Madame Alexandre met Cynthia Levering's eyes and said with deliberate emphasis, "And perhaps many other times as well. I thought you understood that the evening hours were my own. However," she continued icily, "if it puts your mind at ease, I can tell you that I'll only be stopping by to check on *ma tante.*"

Connie smiled. She had come to realize that *ma tante,* if she existed at all, was a woman whose health fluctuated alarmingly, not to say opportunely. Did Miss Levering know that? she wondered. Or was *she* just sensitive to Martine Alexandre because she had become someone it was important for her to understand? For instance, would Martine Alexandre want to maneuver herself into having dinner tonight with George Trevelyan, despite the fact that Diana's presence would make it something less than a tête à tête?

\* \* \*

At dinner that evening, Cynthia Levering relaxed her rule against gossip, and Martine Alexandre, though absent, was paradoxically very present.

"Of course it's hard to tell with foreigners," Miss Levering observed over coffee, "but Madame Alexandre strikes me as very unprofessional. She's very casual about her responsibilities toward the school and toward us."

"*Very* casual," Miss Hardcastle said, shaking her head sorrowfully.

Taking Miss Levering's observation personally, Pervenche Harvitte said firmly, "'Casualness' is hardly typical of the French—if that's what you mean by 'foreigners.' Besides which here in France *we* are the foreigners."

Pervenche then looked at Connie, who wondered whether the astute Frenchwoman had observed that Connie regarded Martine Alexandre as a rival.

"Would you like to go into town for a movie, Connie?" Pervenche asked as they moved away from the table.

Connie considered the suggestion briefly, then said, "No, if you don't mind, I really don't think I feel like it tonight."

It was true. She didn't feel like going into town, but she knew that her decision was based in large part on the fact that she didn't want to take the chance of running into George Trevelyan.

"I think I'll just go upstairs and wash my hair." And wash that man out of my mind at the same time, she determined. The whole day had been spent dreaming about George Trevelyan, and when they had finally met, it wasn't anything like what she had imagined. She'd ruined everything by feeling possessive about a man she had spent two hours and had one phone conversation with! Well, she'd see him tomorrow morning—what on earth would she say to him now that Diana's problems seemed to be solved—and then she'd try to forget him and concentrate on enjoying her summer.

When a knock came at her door several hours later, Connie, who had changed into blue jeans and a comfortable old shirt, assumed it must be Pervenche. "Come in," she called from the bed on which she was lying, a closed book in her lap.

The door opened and George Trevelyan stood on the threshold.

"Oh," said Connie, getting up in confusion. The book fell to the floor, landing at her bare feet. She looked down for a moment in dismay. This was a far cry from the way she had envisioned their meeting. In none of her fantasies had he found her with hair still slightly damp, wearing a pair of patched and faded blue jeans and an old shirt. Her hand moved involuntarily, checking buttons to make sure they were closed, a gesture that did not escape George Trevelyan's notice.

"Have I come at a bad moment?" His voice was light, his glance appreciative.

"Well . . . yes . . . no . . . It's just that I hadn't expected to see you till morning."

"I just brought Diana back, and since our meeting this afternoon was so unsatisfactory. . . . The fact is," he said coolly, "I decided that I wanted to see you right now, that I didn't care to wait until morning." His eyes were glacial as he closed the door behind him and asked sternly, "What was the meaning of that scene, Connie?"

She felt at a disadvantage. She wasn't prepared for him, wasn't prepared for hearing his voice, for sustaining his look. Why did this man have such an effect on her?

"Won't you sit down?" she said with a gesture, defiantly ignoring his question. He had no right to ask for explanations.

Through the open window, Connie could see the full moon, and from the garden below came the rich, suddenly oppressive scent of night-blooming flowers.

Sensing her irritation, George walked past her to the window and said neutrally, "You have a lovely view of the garden, don't you?" Then, his voice caressing her, "It would be wonderful to wake up here in the morning." He turned his eyes full upon her.

"It is wonderful," she said nervously, refusing to acknowledge the possibility of a double meaning in his words. "I've been very happy here."

"You look it. Everything about you shows it." His gray eyes flicked over her appraisingly and she blushed under his gaze.

"You're more beautiful than I remembered," he said slowly. "And I thought I had remembered every detail."

Walking back to where she still stood rooted to the floor, he brushed a damp tendril from her cheek, his fingers moving with slow deliberation, leaving a trail of sensation where they had touched her skin.

"I just washed it," Connie said weakly, aware she was babbling.

Dismissing the remark, he cupped her face in both his hands. They stood there silently, eyes locked, lost in the moment. Connie was breathless; she could feel the blood pounding in her temples, the pulse in her throat beating wildly. As if to quiet it, he lowered his lips to the soft hollow and kissed her gently.

"Still nothing but soap and water?" he said, breathing in her fragrance.

"Still." She laughed. "But the soap is something called Miel d'Abeille. Bees' honey," she explained breathlessly.

"Mmmm," he acknowledged, his mouth moving slowly, deliberately, inexorably to her lips, which warmed under the pressure of his. As his hands slid searchingly down her shoulders and along her body, she became aware of her nakedness under the soft cotton shirt. So did he, and he drew her even closer to him, his warm hands now under her shirt, caressing her skin, his fingertips following each curve of her, the whole length of his body pressing against hers insistently.

In an answering burst of passion that shook her with wonder and delight, she responded by putting her arms around his neck, drawing him ever closer, her full, strangely aching breasts crushed against his hard chest. Raising his lips from hers, he began murmuring in her ear. His voice was hoarse, indistinct, as his hands ceaselessly, demandingly, explored her body.

He began drawing her toward the bed, and the sudden movement broke the spell.

"No," she said, pulling away. "Not this way. Not here." Her denial was full of promise.

At first she thought he hadn't heard, but then slowly, reluctantly, he drew away from her. The empty space between them felt so cold that for a moment she regretted her words. But his arms had slowly dropped to his sides. "Perhaps you're right," he said huskily. "The setting is hardly appropriate."

She could see the undisguised hunger in his eyes, and his face was like a mask etched with the pain of denial.

"I must confess I'm surprised I can feel this way about anybody," he continued thoughtfully. "It's been a long time . . ." He started toward her once more, but stopped as she shook her head, reached out her hand, touched his face lingeringly. "I think you had better go now."

Rigid with the effort to maintain his self-control, he removed her hand from his cheek; he brought it to his lips and kissed the palm hungrily, his eyes never leaving hers.

"I'll see you tomorrow. After breakfast. And tomorrow evening we'll find someplace where we can be alone." His voice was not strong and resolute, and he wheeled around quickly and was gone without waiting for a reply.

She locked the door behind him and leaned against it in a daze. Of all his words, three echoed disturbingly in the empty room. "A long time." What did he mean? His wife had been dead only for a few months.

No! She stilled her sudden disquiet. She had rejected the innuendos of Ann Bennett and the warnings of Pervenche Harvitte; she would trust her instincts. But not for the first time, she wondered what kind of man George Trevelyan really was.

# Chapter Six

When, the following Saturday, George Trevelyan had still not returned to Paris, the school was abuzz with rumor and excitement. The girls had been the first to spot the romance, and chattering little groups could be seen clustered conspiratorially whenever the presumed lovers passed by. The teachers were slower to get wind of it, but when they did, the reaction of at least two of them was one of condemnation.

As Connie and the three Whittier teachers sat at the breakfast table waiting to be served, Miss Levering pursed her lips and said disapprovingly, "Not that anything George Trevelyan could do would surprise me in the least."

"No indeed," Miss Hardcastle gave back faithfully.

Mademoiselle Harvitte remained silent, and Connie obstinately kept her eyes lowered, refusing to meet anyone else's glance.

"But I *had* hoped," Miss Levering continued briskly, "that a person with responsibility for impressionable young girls would have had better sense! It sets such a dreadful example." She stopped abruptly, giving the woman who was waiting on the table time to serve the coffee and croissants and depart. "Even if the man has no respect for the memory of his wife, he should at least have some sensitivity for his daughter's feelings," she continued. Her disapproving tone was genuine; she was profoundly offended on a number of levels. "After all, the poor child's mother has been dead only a few months."

As if daring contradiction, her eyes moved from one to another of her companions, coming to rest on Pervenche Harvitte, who was engaged with the absorption of a chemist in preparing her bowl of café au lait.

"You're very silent this morning, Pervenche. Don't you have any opinion about this so-called romance?"

Carefully setting down the pitcher of hot milk she was holding in one hand and the little pot of coffee that was in the other, Mademoiselle Harvitte replied, with a faraway look, "Only that a woman should take every opportunity for romance that comes her way."

"Of course, you *would* defend her! And what's romance got to do with it? It seems quite obvious that this is more a case of lust than love."

"Aren't you jumping over conclusions?"

"*To* conclusions, Pervenche, *to* conclusions! And no I'm not." Impatiently she turned her attention next to Connie.

"Are you feeling all right? You look a little pale."

"Only a little tired, Miss Levering. It's been a hard week."

"I daresay," replied Miss Levering. "I must tell you, however, that I've been hearing very favorable comments about your music classes from the girls. As a matter of fact, I may sit in one day next week."

Turning to Miss Hardcastle, "Jane, if you've finished your coffee, there's something I'd like to discuss with you in the office."

Miss Hardcastle, who was just about to reach for another croissant, instead hastily gulped down the rest of her café au lait and, pushing back her chair, sprang up like a jack-in-the-box and docilely followed her friend from the room.

As soon as the two were out of earshot, Pervenche Harvitte turned to Connie. "Those cats!"

"What do you mean?" Connie asked listlessly. She looked wan and drawn, and the yellow cotton sheath she was wearing only emphasized her pallor.

"All that talk about George Trevelyan, of course! And she called me a gossip!"

At the sound of his name Connie's hand moved involuntarily to the coral beads at her throat, and she began to finger them nervously. She seemed at a loss for words.

"Of course, though I'd never admit it to Cynthia and Jane, I do think that he and Martine are being a little indiscreet," Pervenche continued. Looking at Connie sympathetically, she added, "I know, *ma chère*, that you found him attractive, but now you can see the kind of man he is."

As she launched into a long dissertation of the curious inability of men to resist the wiles of certain women, her voice formed a background for Connie's thoughts.

It had indeed been a hard week, and the worst thing about it was that none of it made any sense. Heaven knows, she thought bitterly, she had spent enough sleepless nights trying to figure it out. Monday night, she remembered with a stab of pain, she had been in George Trevelyan's arms, and those few moments of rapture had had an intensity she had never before experienced, an urgency that had transported her beyond anything she had ever known. It had been real, real for her and equally real for him. She had been sure—was still sure—of that, and nothing would ever make her change her mind! She had gone to bed happy, knowing she was in love and feeling reasonably sure of being loved in return. And then the next morning there had been his note, the note she had read and reread until it was indelibly engraved on her soul:

I owe you an apology. My behavior was inexcusable. Put it down to too much wine at dinner and please forgive me.

G.

Of course he hadn't shown up after breakfast. How she ever got through her class that morning remained a mystery. She was half-crazed, constantly replaying his every word and gesture, his every kiss and touch, against those three ugly sentences. Was that all it had been? A burst of drunken, undiscriminating sexual passion, which she had been too dazzled to recognize for what it was? Her heart didn't want to believe it, but she had to admit that George Trevelyan hadn't ever mentioned the word *love*.

When she finally saw him later that day he was with Martine Alexandre, and they seemed to be getting along splendidly. He came over when he noticed her, but his manner was remote. "You mentioned on the phone that you had something important to discuss with me?"

She searched his face carefully, looking for a clue, but saw nothing except an unmistakable desire to remain aloof. Was he going to ignore what had happened? In that case, so would she. A pride she had not known she possessed came to her rescue, and she found she was able to match his tone with one equally impersonal. "Yes, I did, but the problem seems to have worked itself out."

"Sometimes they do, if you just give them enough time." He paused, then added cynically, "But then again, sometimes they don't."

Without waiting for a reply, he turned on his heels and walked quickly back to Martine, to whom in the days that followed he had seemed openly, even ostentatiously, attentive. Needless to say, the attractive Frenchwoman reciprocated his interest. In the late afternoons, when Diana was free, he would pick her up and take her for drives, bringing her back to the school for dinner. On at least two occasions he had picked Martine up, and the two of them had gone off for the evening; a sleepless Connie had heard the car returning late those nights.

"Isn't it convenient that Madame Alexandre's aunt has made such a remarkable recovery," Cynthia Levering had commented cynically. "It leaves her free for other things."

What made it so hard, Connie concluded, was that she had to see him every day. He had pulled back from her in Baltimore, too, after their initial attraction, and it had been hard enough to stop thinking about him then; but at least they had both gone their separate ways. It was much harder to put somebody out of your mind when you might run into him at any moment.

As had happened one afternoon when he had come upon her sunbathing in the garden. Wednesday after lunch she had changed into a pair of white denim shorts and a navy-blue halter top, come downstairs, and set the two wicker chairs up facing one another so she could sit in one and put her feet up on the other. Her eyes closed; the warm sun, the fragrant flowers, the occasional trill of a bird, were all so soothing to her jangled nerves that for the first time in two days she was able to put all thoughts of George Trevelyan aside. In fact, she was scarcely thinking at all—she was in such a state of physical contentment that she was practically purring like a cat.

The sound of a snapping twig made her suddenly open her eyes, and she found herself staring up into the face of the man she had finally managed to put from her mind. Something about his posture suggested he had been standing there for a while, and his words confirmed this.

"I suppose I should say I'm sorry for intruding on your privacy, but frankly, I can't regret something that's given me such pleasure."

Indeed there was nothing contrite about his tone.

For two days Connie had been holding imaginary conversations with George Trevelyan, conversations in which she would let him know in no uncertain terms what she thought of his behavior. But now, when the occasion presented itself, her mind was a blank, and all she could think of was to say inanely, "In the short time I've been here, this has become my favorite spot. Isn't it lovely?"

"Lovely," he agreed, staring down at her intently.

His meaning was unmistakable, but instead of pleasing her, it reminded her of her grievances against him, and she determined not to allow herself to be swayed by the power of his charm. If he chose to pretend that nothing had happened between them, she certainly wasn't going to bring it up! Forcing herself to speak in the impersonal tone of someone merely making polite conversation, she asked, "Are you enjoying your stay in Aix?"

"More than I had expected to—and less than I had hoped," he replied enigmatically.

"Really? It's seemed to me as if you had found exactly what you wanted."

His brows darkened, and for a moment she feared an explosion of that fiery temper he had already demonstrated. Instead, he smiled ambiguously and said politely, "Apparently another example of your willingness to believe in appearances."

She was about to reply sharply when he added curtly, "You'll have to excuse me. I've already lingered too long."

His tone was detached and impersonal, but the flickering glance he gave her before turning away was not.

"But we mustn't talk about this now. I see Diana coming over." The sound of Pervenche's voice broke into Connie's musings, and she realized that the Frenchwoman had been talking all this time about George Trevelyan and Martine Alexandre. "I feel sorry for her," Pervenche concluded quickly, "the other girls must be gossiping so."

Diana looked far from an object of pity, though. The truth of the matter was that she was very likely enjoying the reflected glory of the romance that the girls found so exciting.

"Oh, Miss Wyatt, I'm so glad you're still here," said Diana excitedly. "We're going on a drive, and we want you to come with us."

"Who's we?" asked Connie.

"My father and Madame Alexandre. I told him I wanted you to come too."

How ironic! She had won the daughter and lost the father. Her phone call to George Trevelyan in Paris had made an instant fan of Diana, who now wanted to include Connie every time she and her father went for a drive. Luckily, so far it had not been difficult to find excuses.

Connie was about to say "I don't think I can," when Miss Levering returned to the dining room.

"What did Miss Wyatt say?" she asked Diana.

"I don't know yet." The girl turned back to Connie expectantly. "You will come, won't you, Miss Wyatt?"

"Well, I don't know," Connie began slowly, and Miss Levering cut in, her voice brooking no argument.

"But of course you will. It will do you good. You're looking peaked." Turning to Diana, she said, "Run along now. I need to speak to Miss Wyatt."

As Diana hurried out, Cynthia Levering returned to the charge. Her voice was low and intense; what she was saying was obviously important to her. "I'd like to ask you to do this as a favor. I think it's vital to defuse some of the gossip, and I also think it's quite inappropriate for Diana to chaperone her father."

"That's a role I don't much enjoy playing myself," Connie said quickly. "And besides, you did want me to plan the end-of-term entertainment. I've got a lot of work to do on that."

With some surprise, she realized that though she was desperately searching for excuses not to go, perversely there was some small part of her that wanted to.

"In this instance, it's a case of first things first, Connie. This is important for the reputation of the school. I don't want the girls writing to their parents about all the carryings-on here."

"It seems unlikely there would be any carryings-on with Diana along."

"It's not a question of how things are, but of how they look. Your presence will make things *look* much more respectable. I feel very strongly that you must go."

Put that way, it was obvious that there was nothing more Connie could say, and resignedly she went upstairs to get ready.

The outing was just as bad as she had feared. Diana had insisted that she sit with her in the back of the convertible—not that there was much choice, since Martine was already firmly planted up front next to George. There was something about sitting in the back seat that always made Connie feel like a child; all the decisions—where to go, how to get there, when to stop—were made by the grownups in front, while the children in the back were supposed to amuse themselves quietly. That was obviously what it was going to be like today, and her feeling of being the powerless child was only heightened as she noted the contrast between her own simple yellow dress and Martine Alexandre's elegant and sophisticated beige silk pongee outfit, accented by a long strand of beautiful jade beads that disappeared provocatively into her décolletage.

"Did I understand you to say that there were bullfights in Marseilles?" George's question was directed to Martine.

"Indeed there are. I know most people think you have to go to Spain to see bullfights, but fortunately we sometimes have them right here in Marseilles. As a matter of fact, there's one scheduled for today. Why don't we go? I simply adore bullfights."

"How do you two like that idea?" George glanced in the rear view mirror at the occupants of the back seat.

Connie's reaction was immediate. "I don't like bullfights!"

"Ah, but that's only because you don't understand them." Martine Alexandre turned around in her seat and focused her attention on Connie for the first time. Even in the open car, Connie noticed, the cloud of Joy in which Martine had drenched herself was overpowering.

"It's a very beautiful ritual, very classic. And it's not at all as unfair as you may think. The strength of the bull is pitted against the intelligence and skill of the matador." Her eyes were bright with an almost sexual excitement. "And you never know which one will win."

Connie, her voice full of quiet outrage, snapped back immediately, "But the one thing you do know is that the end result is death—for one or the other."

Madame Alexandre shrugged impatiently. "You Americans will never learn about life until you learn to deal with death."

The silence that followed as the others considered this statement was finally broken, again by Connie. "I *have* dealt with death, and though I am not afraid of it, I see no reason to seek it out or to glorify it."

George Trevelyan turned around and met Connie's eyes. "We *all* have, haven't we?" he murmured gravely; then turning back to the woman beside him, he said briskly, "Perhaps the bullfight isn't such a good idea, Martine. Let's think of something else."

Martine seemed about to argue the point, but suppressed the impulse and, resting a beautifully manicured hand on George Trevelyan's arm, said, "Whatever you think best, George. I'll be completely guided by you."

This geishalike deference was totally out of keeping with Martine Alexandre's style at the school, but so far as Connie could see, George Trevelyan was absolutely lapping it up.

"What about Avignon?" he said after some thought.

"That's a good idea," Martine agreed. "We can stop at Arles first and see some of the Roman ruins, then spend the afternoon in Avignon."

"Remember the song, Diana?" George Trevelyan began to sing, *"Sur le pont d'Avignon, on y danse, on y danse, tout en ronde."*

The musician in Connie was not surprised by the fine baritone. His voice was the first thing she had noticed about him.

"Oh yes," Diana replied eagerly. "We learned that in third grade! Is there really a bridge in Avignon?"

"There certainly is," her father replied, "but after eight hundred years there's not much of it left. It ends partway across the Rhône. You'll see."

Following some consultation of the map, which seemed to require more physical contact between George Trevelyan and Martine Alexandre than Connie would have thought necessary, they wended their way along country roads bordered by rows of tall, straight poplars and cypresses, beyond which lay endless vineyards and groves of gnarled olive trees. Connie was glad for the distraction of the landscape, since the almost inevitable separation between the occupants of the front seat and the back seat was reinforced by Martine Alexandre's lack of interest in including either her or Diana in her remarks to George Trevelyan. Occasionally their heads would almost touch as they exchanged an inaudible comment; it hurt so much to watch that Connie tried to close her eyes against the sight, but Diana's affectionate chatter made such a retreat almost impossible. All she could do was hope that there would be a reshuffling when they got to Arles.

But Martine Alexandre proved tenacious, and George Trevelyan seemed content with things as they were, or at least he made no protest. Throughout the morning's sightseeing, it was George and Martine, Connie and Diana—up and down the steps of the ancient arena, in and out of the ruins of the old forum, back and forth along the melancholy pathways of Alyscamps, the famous early Christian necropolis.

Only at lunch were they together, and then just superficially, for even when they were all sharing the same table, Martine bent all her effort toward creating the impression that she and George were a unit.

Sometimes her behavior became so obviously proprietary that George would pointedly address a remark to his daughter or deliberately meet Connie's eyes. He would ask Connie's opinion about something, start a conversation, but almost as deliberately pull himself away. Martine's campaign was apparently succeeding. With a sigh, Connie conceded that George must indeed prefer the company of the more sophisticated older woman. It was going to be a long day.

Long and difficult. Connie had always hated finding herself in situations where she was not free to come and go as she pleased, and when they returned to the car to continue on their way to Avignon, she felt exactly like a prisoner.

"Perhaps Diana would like to sit in the front seat," she suggested, eager to try to put a crimp in Martine's takeover of the day. But before George could answer, Martine cut in. "Since we're going by back roads and I know the way, I think it's best that I remain up front."

And that ended that.

Avignon. The scene of the "Babylonian Captivity," when the popes were under the thumb of the French, reminded Connie of her own situation. Only the thought of the kindly Pervenche Harvitte kept her from absolutely loathing all the French—at least all French women—at this point. They toured the Pope's Palace, and Connie paused by herself for a moment at a window to look out over the burnt sienna–tiled roofs of the town. It was lovely, she had to admit, moved almost in spite of herself.

Later, as they all stood on a terrace overlooking the famous bridge, she had her first opportunity that day to talk to George privately. Martine had chosen that moment to be ostentatiously charming to Diana, whom she had previously rigorously ignored.

Connie and George contemplated the four arches that advanced into the river before the bridge ended abruptly.

"There's something very moving about that fragment of bridge. It starts out so firmly, so sure of where it's going, and then it finds itself right in the middle of nowhere, broken and of no use to anyone." His usually vibrant voice had a faraway and distant sound, and though he was speaking of the bridge, it was obvious that he was thinking of something else.

A surge of irritation rose in Connie. "I suppose there's something romantically melancholy about it, like all ruins, but I can't help feeling that there's also something willful in the decision not to restore it. Right now everything in me is itching to make that bridge do what a bridge is supposed to do—link up with the other side. Fragments can be made whole, you know. They've restored everything else around here, including that arena in Arles, which goes back to Roman times and must have been in worse shape than this!" Her voice sounded sharp to her ears and she continued more quietly. "Now the arena is a part of the town's everyday life, something that living people use."

Like George Trevelyan, she was talking about the bridge but thinking about something else. In some undefined way, she was struggling with him, trying desperately to reach him, to make him understand what she had just begun to understand herself.

She had given up the hope of his loving her, and she was trying to stop loving him, but she had had a lot of time to think about this man. She thought about his moodiness, the way his attitude toward her oscillated between extreme attraction and total indifference, his arrogance and self-assurance—and about the more vulnerable side of him she had glimpsed in Baltimore. She was sure she understood one thing: he must have loved his wife very much indeed to be so mired in the past. She felt that for some reason she brought out that aspect of his personality.

Startled by her outburst, he stood there rigid at first; then his piercing gray eyes looked at her long and hard, and when he spoke his voice was harsh. "There are some things that cannot be mended, that belong irrevocably to the past." He added angrily, "You're too young to understand."

Before she had a chance to answer, Martine Alexandre came up, and, placing a proprietary hand on his arm, she said, "You know, George, there's a fine inn nearby, and since we cannot get Diana and Connie back to school in time for dinner, I suggest we just stay on and eat here."

It took Connie a moment to understand what Martine was saying. Every time she spoke to George Trevelyan she was brought to depths of feeling that left her trembling—with rage, with frustration, with longings she had no words for. Now her heart sank. She wanted nothing so much as to get back to school, to get away from all of them, and she couldn't. Diana, unfortunately, was delighted with Martine's idea, and George quickly concurred. There was no way out. In other circumstances, Connie would have been able to plead a previous engagement, but here in France, and living at the school as she did, that was impossible. Nevertheless, she played the only card she had.

"Miss Levering probably expected us back by now—"

But Martine Alexandre immediately overrode this objection. "Nonsense. Diana's with her father, and you're both with me."

"You needn't feel responsible for me," Connie said rebelliously. Martine's earlier remark about getting "Connie and Diana" back in time for dinner had infuriated her, but this clear statement of the hierarchy was too much to let pass.

Sensing the barely contained friction between the two women, George Trevelyan broke in. "I noticed an interesting-looking square near the Pope's Palace. Perhaps we can all stop in a café and have an aperitif."

"Oh yes," said Martine, literally turning her back on Connie. "Place de l'Horloge. That's the center of town." As she proceeded to lead them there, she explained that the Avignon summer drama festival was underway, which was why the town was so crowded. The square was particularly lively. Performing magicians, jugglers, and musicians of all kinds attracted groups made up almost equally of elegantly dressed tourists and sandaled students; crowds milled around the stands of foods, local crafts, and jewelry. They stopped to watch a young man who was doing amazing things with nothing but a pair of scissors and enormous sheets of paper, folding and cutting them to make lacy creations of elaborate complexity that he exhibited with a flourish to general applause. When the hat was passed, George Trevelyan contributed generously.

At the café Martine Alexandre ordered a *pastis,* and Connie was instantly reminded of her first day on the Cours Mirabeau. She thought of the dazzlingly handsome Frenchman who had shared her table, and was struck by the contrast in the way she had felt then and how she felt now. Last week she had been made to feel very attractive, very desirable, a woman to be courted rather than carted about. Now she felt like something between a babysitter and a fifth wheel.

As the waiter deposited their drinks, Martine Alexandre suddenly leaned across the table and took George Trevelyan's left hand in hers. "What an unusual ring. I've been admiring it for days."

The easy gesture aroused a mixture of envy and

admiration in Connie, who recalled her own stifled impulse to do just the same thing that day in Baltimore.

"It's a moonstone, isn't it?" Martine asked. "And it's carved, but I can't make it out. What is it?" Her hand was still on his.

"It's the Trevelyan crest, a garlanded oak. The ring is a family heirloom. It's been handed down to the oldest son for five generations now."

"So your family has always been wealthy—I mean, socially prominent," she said, quickly reorienting her thrust.

Connie looked over to see if George had reacted in any way, but his face was impassive; though he had withdrawn his hand, she was pleased to note. Mostly he seemed at a loss as to how to reply.

He shrugged. "The Trevelyans have been around for a long time, but you know, there's always a horsethief or a con man back there someplace. It doesn't pay to check too closely."

"Why are you always so reluctant to admit social distinctions? After all, money and social position are the basis of all culture."

"I don't know that I agree with that. In any case, they are also responsible for a lot of superficial nonsense."

Connie, who had been listening and watching attentively, began to understand why Ed Hamilton thought so highly of George Trevelyan. She liked the simplicity and honesty with which he had handled Martine's question, just as she admired the way he had never made an issue about his wealth or importance. If only he could be open about other matters . . . about his sudden change of heart where she was concerned, for example.

Then, almost as though laying a trap for her, Martine Alexandre turned abruptly to Connie and included her in the conversation for the first time. "Don't *you* think that money and social position are important, Connie?"

After a moment's consideration, Connie replied, "What's important is what you do with them, I imagine."

As she said this she looked toward George and found he was watching her intently. "You know," she went on, meeting his gaze steadily, "Mr. Hamilton has told me how much time and effort you contributed to some of the restoration projects in Baltimore. He said they couldn't have done it without your help and advice, that you were the one impartial voice of reason."

"That's one of the benefits of wealth, you know. It's easy to be objective when you have nothing to gain or lose." His tone was offhand, casual. But Connie, observing him carefully, could see that he was pleased.

Martine, however, was not, and obviously regretted having drawn Connie into the conversation. Never one to lose the initiative for very long, she said to George, "I think we should perhaps start for the inn now, if we want to be sure of getting a table." And as they rose from their seats, she reestablished her claim to George Trevelyan by casually linking her arm with his during the walk back to the car.

L'Auberge des Papes proved to be a real inn, not just a restaurant. It was in a secluded spot, several kilometers outside of town. The sun was just setting as they parked near a clear, swiftly flowing stream, and the light had a special quality, what Pervenche had described earlier that week as *"entre chien et loup"*— when you couldn't tell a dog from a wolf. In a garden alongside the rambling two-story house tables had been set up, and on each one there were tiny earthenware jugs of fresh wildflowers illuminated by hurricane lamps that cast a romantic glow. Chinese lanterns hung from the trees, and the soft murmur of conversation filled the air.

"How enchanting!" Connie exclaimed spontaneously, forgetting for a moment her intense desire to be back in the security of her room.

The meal enhanced the initial favorable impression. It began with a wonderful coarse country pâté served with *tart cornichons,* and went on to a *daube de mouton à la provençale*—marinated lamb surrounded by small white onions in a sauce redolent of bay leaves and fresh tomatoes. The salad that followed, they were told, had just been picked from the vegetable garden that afternoon, and the carafe of local wine that George had decided upon proved to be a happy choice. Diana, who had been lured away from the table by the discovery of a litter of kittens, came back in time to choose her dessert—an apricot tart—while the others decided on fresh strawberries served with a heaping bowl of crème chantilly.

Despite the tensions of the day, the dinner induced in all of them a state of euphoria, which quickly vanished when they returned to the car and discovered that it wouldn't start.

After talking to the innkeeper, they learned they would not be able to get a mechanic till morning, and for a moment they all stood there indecisively.

"Well, I see nothing to do but take rooms here for the night," George said finally. "Assuming we can get them."

"Let's settle that right away," said Martine, who didn't look at all displeased at the change in plan.

But what appeared to be an adventure for her was to Connie only the prolongation of an ordeal. She didn't welcome the idea of spending the night under the same roof as George Trevelyan, or the prospect of another day like this one. Yet there seemed nothing to do about it but accept the situation as gracefully as possible.

They all went inside and were told that if Diana would take the little room downstairs—not too far from that litter of kittens, the innkeeper laughed—he could put the rest of them in the three remaining rooms upstairs.

"While George and I are arranging for the rooms, Connie," said Martine authoritatively, "why don't you phone the school?" Again Connie bridled at the tone, but she was too tired to make an issue of it and wordlessly nodded her agreement.

Cynthia Levering's response when Connie explained the situation indicated a total lack of surprise. "Well, perhaps now you understand why I felt it imperative that someone go along."

"But who knew this was going to happen? It was totally unforeseen!"

"I was quite sure that something 'unforeseen' would happen," was Miss Levering's parting shot.

Connie was still wondering about what that meant as she walked back to her room from the bathroom down the corridor. The inn was larger than it looked from the outside: George Trevelyan's room was at the far end of a long corridor, and she and Martine Alexandre had adjoining rooms at the other end. None of the rooms had a private bath, but at least they all had sinks, and closing the door behind her—she noticed that it didn't have a lock—Connie gratefully washed and began to get ready for bed.

She would, she realized, have to sleep in the nude, since of course she had nothing with her—not even a toothbrush; thinking with dismay of the next morning, she grimaced. Oh, well, at least they were all in the same boat.

Feeling curiously vulnerable, she slid between the

coarse but immaculate sheets that smelled faintly of lavender, but the sensation was quickly lost as a wave of exhaustion overtook her. It was wonderful to lie down. The day had been so draining—emotionally if not physically—that she was asleep almost at once and so had no idea how much time had passed when she was roused by a fumbling at her door.

As the doorknob turned softly, she instinctively drew the sheets protectively around her. Every atom of her being knew who was standing on the other side of that door. It had to be George Trevelyan, and she was guiltily aware that the tremor that went through her was not just fear.

Angry at her own response, she called out firmly, "Go away!"

The doorknob was instantly released and the latch clicked back into place. Then there was the sound of footsteps, and the door to the room next to hers opened and quietly closed.

Sitting up in bed, she kicked off the sheet. Her body was burning with the double humiliation of knowing that she had wanted him to insist, to plead—and that he had preferred to do neither. There was no doubt in her mind that George Trevelyan had just entered Martine Alexandre's room.

# Chapter Seven

She felt herself pinned to the bed, her lips being sought urgently. A man lay with his full weight on her, and, writhing under him, she tried to free herself. Reaching out blindly in the dark, she clawed at him and with a desperate burst of energy she wrenched her head to one side and saw in the shaft of moonlight a hand bearing a curiously carved signet ring. She recognized the garlanded oak.

The sound of her own strangled cry rang in her ears when she sat up in bed. Her legs were drawn up tightly against her body, her chestnut hair tumbling wildly about her shoulders; she was shaken by a long, uncontrollable shudder. It had all been so real that it took a few moments to realize that it was only a dream. A dream that had left her with a curiously aching void, an intense longing. She raised her head and stared unseeingly into the darkness of the room.

It didn't take a psychoanalyst, she thought ruefully, to figure out the meaning of that dream, or the nature of what she had wanted. She had to face it—she loved George Trevelyan, and that love wasn't going to disappear just because he didn't share her feelings. Why hadn't anyone ever told her that love could be like this? That it need not start with friendship and understanding and slowly develop into intimacy, but that it could happen in a blinding flash, as it had to her that afternoon in Mt. Vernon Place; that it could continue to exist in the face of a relationship that swung between extremes of total unity and comprehension and just as total indifference and misunderstanding; that it could humiliate her to the extent that she had to admit that the one she loved might at that very moment have another woman in his arms.

Brooding about these conflicting emotions, trying to reestablish a sense of emotional equilibrium, Connie spent the rest of the night sleeping only fitfully, and it was with a sense of relief that she finally saw the sky beginning to lighten. Reluctant to make any noise so early in the morning, she tiptoed to the sink and proceeded to give herself a makeshift sponge bath. Then with a resigned shrug, she picked up the clothes she had discarded the night before and swiftly dressed, muttering under her breath, "Darn Miss Levering! Darn Martine Alexandre! And make it a double for George Trevelyan!"

She felt disheveled and at a disadvantage, even more so today than the day before. But at least today there was no longer any confusion in her mind. Yesterday, despite her unwillingness to be included in the outing, some small part of her still held hope. Until she could talk to George Trevelyan, until he said to her face what he had said in his note—not until then would she believe that it was really over, over before it had even had a chance to begin. "Too much wine" indeed! Not for one moment did she believe that! But on the other hand she didn't know what she *should* believe. She had to talk to him. There was no other way.

Well, they had had a few moments together, had even begun to talk, and in that time she thought she had a glimpse of what must be bothering him. In part it had something to do with youth, but there had to be more to it than that. Whatever it was that she had sensed in him in Baltimore was evident again yesterday. Unfortunately, with her flawless timing, Martine Alexandre had once again managed to come between them. And though Connie knew George had been more aware of her, more concerned for her for the rest of the day, it was to Martine that he had turned at night. All right, she got the message. Come what may, she would insist they return to school right after breakfast.

Not wanting to encounter either of the occupants of the other room, Connie stood warily by the door, listening. She had not heard him leave, and she felt sure she would have. They must both still be asleep, she concluded. After a few moments' silence, during which she heard nothing, she decided the coast was clear and hurried downstairs. Confident that she would be the first in the dining room, it came as a shock to Connie to find George, now in his role of fond father, already at breakfast with Diana. How had he managed to get downstairs without her hearing him?

To her chagrin, the sight of him embarrassed her, and she almost turned to leave. But as she watched him, still unaware of her presence, looking remarkably relaxed, a wave of anger swept over her. It was he, not she, who should be embarrassed. After all, he had no way of knowing about her dream. . . .

Clearly, however, he wasn't. George Trevelyan's lean, handsome face reflected only pleasure as he rose from his seat and pulled out a chair for her. "Good morning, Connie." His eyes, which so accurately mirrored his moods, were friendly and admiring, his voice warm and welcoming. "Judging by your looks, you must have had a better bed than I did. Or is it just another advantage of being young?"

Before Connie could answer, Diana piped up, "Hi! I'm just about to go see the kittens. Don't you want to come with me?"

"I think I'll have some breakfast first, Diana. Maybe I'll join you later."

As Diana bounded off, Connie said wryly, "If there is any advantage to youth, Diana is the only one here young enough to enjoy it."

Struck by this remark, George said slowly, "She *does* seem to be enjoying herself, doesn't she? I'm glad to see her so carefree; she hasn't had a very happy time of it. She—" He stopped abruptly.

Connie said nothing, waiting for him to continue, but when he remained silent, she plunged in. "Yes, her mother's death must have been a terrible shock to her."

He seemed not to hear. His eyes were on her arm, and as she looked down to follow his gaze, he ran his fingers gently over her skin. "Have you been playing with the kittens, too?"

"What?" Connie asked blankly; then, seeing the faint scratches on her arm, she remembered her dream and felt the blood rush to her face. For one insane moment, she was sure he could read her mind. "I guess . . . I guess I must have. . . ."

"Perhaps you're not as awake as I thought," he teased. His voice was amused, but in a nice way— protective, caring. "Here, let me get you some coffee, and try a brioche. The food is so good it almost makes up for those lumpy beds."

"Thank you," she said coolly. Steeling herself against the effect he always had on her, she carefully spread gooseberry jam on the brioche as if the act required all her powers of concentration.

Considering where he had spent the night, Connie felt the topic of beds was more than she could handle. "The real problem for me was having to get into these clothes again. I feel so messy."

George Trevelyan leaned back in his chair and ran his eyes over her, then said judiciously, "You don't *look* that way at all, I assure you." He smiled a lopsided smile, then looked at her face again more searchingly, and frowned. "No, you don't look messy, but your eyes—your eyes look tired."

His concern was genuine and Connie was touched, then irritated. If her eyes were tired, it was in large measure because of him! Before she could answer, he was speaking again.

"I suppose I should thank you for coming on this trip. I won't pretend I don't know that you were reluctant to." He paused, but kept his gaze steady on hers and added in a voice so low she could barely hear it, "Or why."

A wave of exultation swept over Connie. This was what she had been waiting for—he had broached the subject. But perversely, still enraged by the openness of his liaison with Martine Alexandre, she ignored the opening, picking up only the first part of what he had said. "Well, I had a lot of work to do planning for our end-of-term entertainment."

"I may be lots of things, Connie," he retorted sharply, "but I'm not a fool!" His tone softened. "However, if you prefer not to discuss this, we won't."

He waited for her to say something, but she remained stubbornly silent, playing nervously with her cup, refusing to meet his eyes. Leaning across the table, he held her hands in his powerful grip. "Look at me!" Not until she raised her eyes to his did he continue, speaking slowly, deliberately. "There have been decided advantages—for me, at least—to your having

117

been along on this trip." He smiled sardonically. "I've been thinking of what you said yesterday about the bridge, though it wasn't the bridge you were talking about, was it?"

"No, it wasn't." This time she answered him directly, without hesitation. Despite all the evidence to the contrary, it was obvious that they were still capable of operating on the same wavelength. From their first conversation in Mt. Vernon Place it had been clear that there was the possibility of almost total communication between them. When they spoke, he seemed to understand what she meant better—or at least more clearly—than she did herself, and part of her pleasure in his company was the joy of that shared connection. He *had* understood what she was talking about yesterday. What had he made of it?

"I have a temper, Connie." The acknowledgment did not appear to embarrass him. "And no doubt I sometimes overreact."

"Indeed you do," she murmured. "I noticed that the very first time I saw you in the Lexington Market."

They smiled at each other like old friends, sharing a pleasant memory. Then he continued, serious once more, *"Usually* when I get angry it's because I'm hearing something I don't want to hear. That was true yesterday. But the more I thought about it, the more I realized you were right. Perhaps I've been stupid in focusing on the past instead of on the present."

"I guess everyone tends to do that." Connie tried to concentrate on what to say, but she was conscious only of her hands still clasped in his. "That's why I came to Aix, you know—to make a real change and to experience myself in new surroundings. I felt it was the only way I could find out what I really wanted to do from here on in."

"And do you think you know?" he asked, looking at her challengingly.

"Perhaps not what I want to do—though I find I enjoy teaching—but I've learned some things about myself that I didn't know before." Including, she thought, a hunger for physical fulfillment that had only recently been discovered.

"Yes, I too thought that I knew myself. Recognized my limits. Understood what I could do, what I could have—and what I would have to live without." His gray eyes had clouded over and focused on the distance as he spoke these enigmatic words. Then they returned to meet Connie's steady gaze and became as icy as his voice. He continued, "And until recently I've been able to manage quite adequately within these limits. But I've also learned something about myself this week." Again he paused; his grip on her hands tightened, and he went on in a rush. "You know, Connie, that night in your room—that note I sent you—"

But Connie was not to hear the end of that sentence.

"What a wonderful morning! I'm sorry if I've kept you waiting, but it took some time to arrange for a bath." Martine Alexandre made her entrance looking bandbox-fresh, not so much as a wrinkle in her dress, her hair in a perfect French twist.

Martine had an unerring talent for spoiling things where she was concerned, Connie thought bitterly, her deep disappointment at being interrupted at this particular moment compounded by her annoyance at Martine's exquisite grooming. She wished it had occurred to her to arrange for a bath, but she hadn't even seen evidence of a tub anywhere.

"Did you all sleep well?" Martine asked brightly. "I had a simply marvelous night myself." She flashed a smile in George's direction.

The only redeeming feature of this interruption, Connie thought, was that George seemed to find it as irritating as she did. But perhaps he was only angered by Martine's obviousness about what had happened the night before.

"Am I interrupting something?" Martine's tone was light, but her eyes were sharply appraising, resting for a long minute on their joined hands. Connie made a move to free hers, but George, without looking at her, merely held them tighter. Martine's eyes met Connie's, and in that brief glance Connie knew that Martine was seeing her for the first time as a rival worthy of consideration.

"Not at all," George said politely, now releasing Connie's hands and once more rising. "We were just waiting for you. Connie would like to get back to Aix as soon as possible."

"My goodness, whatever for? After all it's Sunday, there's no reason to get back early today. And in any case I've had a wonderful idea. A friend of mine has a ceramics studio in an old farmhouse near Cavaillon, and I thought we might stop there. You'll find it interesting, and I know she'll be pleased to meet you."

"I think not, Martine. Not this time," George replied firmly.

Martine shrugged and turned to Connie. "You poor dear. Did you sleep so badly?" Without waiting for an answer, she continued, "By the way, I must apologize for disturbing you last night. At one point I mistook your door for mine."

Connie involuntarily glanced at George to see how he was reacting to this effort to cover up last night's escapade, but his face told her nothing. And then it hit her: Martine, of all women, would make no attempt to cover up anything. In fact, she would be much more likely to flaunt her conquest before Connie in triumph.

No, she was telling the truth; it had *not* been George who had mistaken her door and then gone on his way! That whole scenario had been nothing but the convoluted product of her own imagination. Her sense of relief was overwhelming.

"No, I went right back to sleep." Connie wondered if that could pass as just a "white" lie. "But I really do have to get back, Martine."

Before Martine could raise any further objections, Diana came bursting in. "Oh, Dad! I love those kittens, and I just hate to leave them," she said mournfully.

Observing Diana's crestfallen look, Martine moved in at once. "You know, Diana, I have a friend living near here. She has cats—and a flock of sheep! There are sure to be some baby lambs too. I had thought we might stop there and pay her a little visit, but Miss Wyatt wants to go back to the school immediately."

"Oh, no! Must we, Miss Wyatt? Can't we stop for just a little while?"

"Now, Diana, don't pester Miss Wyatt. If she says she has to get back, she has to get back," George interjected sharply.

Well aware of Martine's ploy, Connie nonetheless felt it would be unkind to deny Diana such a simple pleasure. "I guess if Cavaillon is on the way . . ." She wavered.

"But of course it is," Martine replied.

"Oh, good!" Diana said excitedly. "Then we *can* stop! That's great, Miss Wyatt. Thanks a lot."

"Are you sure, Connie?" George asked. "You mustn't let yourself be imposed upon."

"I'll remember your words in the future, but right now another hour or two won't make any difference."

The looks exchanged between George and Connie did not escape the watchful Martine, who again looked speculatively at her and then said briskly, "Well, that's settled. I'll just have a cup of coffee, and we can leave immediately."

Although the seating arrangements in the car were the same as those of the day before, the atmosphere was totally different. Today it was George who was in control; perfectly polite to Martine, he nevertheless made his displeasure at her exaggerated air of proprietorship quite clear, and established Connie's inclusion in the group beyond question. Eventually even Martine acknowledged the change by making an effort to include Connie in her remarks.

Turning in her seat, she said, "My friend, Janine Alain, is a very remarkable woman. For many years she and her husband ran the ceramics studio together. We have a few of their things in the dining room at school. Then several years ago, without any warning, he walked out on her. Just like that. After twenty years together, he suddenly told her one morning, "I'm leaving! I want my life back!" Martine's tone indicated that she found the story amusing.

"How awful for her!" Connie's response was immediate.

"It's simply to be expected." Martine's voice was casual. "After all, men are polygamous by instinct and monogamous only for the sake of domestic convenience. When Pierre left her, he was just reverting to type."

No one challenged her calculatedly provocative statement, and she continued, "At first, of course, Janine was crushed. But Pierre's leaving turned out to be the best thing in the world for her."

"How so?" George asked, his interest tinged with mockery.

"Well, up until that point, people had thought that it was Pierre who was the talented one. He did the art pieces while poor Janine did the bread and butter things—you know, the ashtrays, the tea sets, the jewelry."

"Then what happened?" Connie asked, caught up in spite of herself.

"Well, I think it's quite ironic," said Martine with a little laugh. "Being free of him set her free artistically. Now *she's* the one who's quite famous here. Once she had pulled herself together, it became apparent that what had seemed the breaking of her was actually the making of her!"

"So she built herself a new life," George said speculatively. Looking up, his eyes met Connie's in the mirror.

"There's no such thing as a *new* life," Martine said flatly. "There's just life, and you take advantage of whatever you can to make it more pleasant."

Connie's reply was immediate, and she realized it was as much in opposition to Martine as it was an expression of her own feelings, although she hadn't thought much about these things until very recently. "But there is such a thing as a new *attitude* toward life, isn't there?" Connie felt as though the dialogue begun at the breakfast table was still going on.

Martine caught something in the wind and glanced interestedly from Connie to George. Whatever she intuited, she decided to let the conversation drop, and they rode in silence.

"That's it!" Martine said a few minutes later, pointing to a sign by a low rambling house at the left of the road. " 'Les Deux Colombes'—though one of the doves has long since flown the nest." Her light, sophisticated laugh was an invitation to the others to share her amusement, but no one did.

No sooner had the car turned into the short driveway

than the door of the house opened and a sturdily built woman wearing a blue artist's smock came to the doorway, shading her eyes against the blinding provençal sun.

*"Janine! C'est moi, Martine!"*

With a cry of genuine pleasure, the woman ran toward the car. *"Oh, Martine! Quel plaisir!"*

The two women embraced, and as Martine disengaged herself, she explained, "I've brought some American friends with me. I hope you don't mind."

"Mind! Of course not, I'm delighted." Janine spoke now in English, turning to the others with a warmly welcoming smile.

Connie observed her with interest. Janine Alain was an amply built woman in her early forties. Her strong features were softened by a halo of casually cut curly gray hair and there were crinkly laugh lines at the corners of her flashing brown eyes. As she shook hands with Connie her grip was firm and warm, her hands strong and capable looking. Janine Alain was the kind of woman more accurately described as "handsome" than beautiful. There was a forthright quality about her that Connie liked immediately. She found it difficult to conceive of this woman as being a friend of Martine Alexandre's; they seemed worlds apart.

"We stopped by to see your work, Janine." The chic Martine, looking like a bird of paradise in these rural surroundings, put a hand on Diana's shoulder. "And I told Diana here that you were sure to have some baby lambs."

"I certainly do," Janine said with a smile. "They're in the pasture behind the barn. We'll go find them in a moment, all right?" Then, turning to Martine, she continued, "How remarkable that you should come by today. I was just going to call you. Michel turned up this morning. He's driven off somewhere now, but he should be back any minute. You know how he is—he comes and goes without any explanation."

Martine frowned. For the first time since Connie had met her, she seemed disconcerted. "George," she said in a falsely bright tone, "why don't you and Connie take a look around the studio? Janine won't mind, will you?"

"Of course not," Janine said. "Who knows, perhaps I'll even make a sale."

They all laughed, and then Martine continued, "I'll join you in a little while; but first I have something I must talk to Janine about. We will take Diana down to see the lambs."

George and Connie looked at each other, surprised at this sudden gift of privacy; even the loyal Janine seemed a little bewildered, but since Martine had already started to walk away with Diana in tow, Janine shrugged and moved to catch up with them.

"I wonder what that's all about," George said in puzzled amusement. "Well, never mind. Let's take advantage of it." He looked down at Connie and then deliberately put his arm around her and guided her through the studio door.

They stood for a minute or two, letting their eyes adjust to the contrast between the harsh light outside and the dimness of the low, cool room. A potter's wheel sat in the center, and against the whitewashed stucco walls were long tables heaped with molds, mounds of tiles, and row upon row of ceramic objects of all sizes, shapes, and colors, some already fired, some waiting for the oven. The riot of color and design was such that it was hard to know where to turn first, but a series of brilliantly colored plaques resting on one of the tables caught Connie's eye.

"I wonder what those are?" she asked, slipping away from George's encircling arm and going toward them. From where they had been standing, the designs on the plaques were not distinguishable; and by the time Connie got close enough to see exactly what those shapes were, it was too late to ignore them. The depictions of lovemaking were very explicit—every conceivable variation of man and woman together. There was no attempt at photographic realism, but there was also no mistaking the atmosphere of blatant sensuality. In all of them an orange noonday sun blazed over erotically entwined bodies; the borders were decorated with heavy clusters of grapes or sheaves of ripened wheat. The golden figures were all in high relief, begging to be touched—but Connie did not dare.

It reminded her of a time when she was about ten years old, and her father had taken her to an exhibition of Renaissance paintings. There was one of a naked Venus and Adonis that had embarrassed her terribly. When her father noted her discomfort, he had said gently, "Connie, you're too young to understand, but always remember that there is nothing shameful in nature."

She knew this was true, but even so . . .

"Obviously our friend Janine has chosen to celebrate the pleasures of love in the afternoon. I'm glad to see that being abandoned by her husband hasn't soured her view of life." George's voice was so close that Connie was startled.

As he leaned forward to pick up one of the plaques, his shoulder brushed against hers. The room had become unnaturally still. She could hear the soft buzzing of the bees outside, and she was conscious of the sound of his breathing.

Mesmerized, Connie watched as he ran his fingers

lovingly over a female figure lying in a position of complete abandon. It seemed to her as if his hand were running along the length of her own body, and she wondered if this thought was in his mind as well. It must have been, for the next thing she knew, he had put the plaque down and had caught her in his arms. His mouth came down on hers hungrily, and she found herself responding with equal passion, forgetting everything but his strong body against hers.

Then suddenly, drawing on all her strength, she pushed both hands against his chest and broke from his embrace.

"How dare you! How dare you assume that you have the right to come and go in and out of my life just as you please!"

His face mirrored his surprise. "What's wrong?"

"Perhaps that's something I should ask you. I don't understand you at all. Don't you know that you can't go around turning people on and off? If your note meant what I had to assume it meant, then I don't understand your behavior now! What am I? Your Sunday woman?" Connie couldn't hide her bitterness, and her voice was relentless as she concluded, each word distinct and clear, *"What do you want?"*

"I should think that would be obvious enough," he replied huskily. "I want *you.* I want you more than I've ever wanted anyone in my life. I tell you, you've reached me in ways that no one ever has before." His gray eyes burned into hers as he repeated firmly, *"No one!"*

But before Connie could rejoice in this admission he continued. "Why pretend? Why deny what you know you want? Surely this isn't the first time—"

Connie's hand flew toward his cheek but was easily intercepted.

"Isn't that gesture just a shade Victorian?" His voice was bitter, mocking.

"Perhaps, but then you're behaving rather like a Victorian villain." Enraged, she managed to wrench her hand from his iron grasp. "And suppose you tell me just what there would be for me in such an arrangement?"

"Pleasure."

"What if I want happiness?"

"You may not always have the choice." He continued, his voice icy with contempt, "I regret that they are by no means synonymous; I suspect they may not even be compatible."

"If pleasure is what you wanted, why did you send me that note? It was hardly calculated to make me fall into your arms."

He made no reply.

"Surely you could see that the maiden had been completely dazzled," she continued with a mock curtsy, "and that you were well on your way to having your will with her?"

"I admit to having displayed some infirmness of purpose," he said, his usual self-assurance momentarily shaken. "Perhaps that admission will be of some consolation to you. But surely you understood that there wasn't a word of truth in that note?"

Her heart seized at these words, but she was not to be deflected. "Then why?"

"A man gets tired of playing the villain," he said wearily. Then in a different tone he added, "You seemed so young, so trusting, and I realized I wasn't ready to make any commitments."

"Not even to Martine?" The words were out before she could curb them.

"Martine and I are two of a kind."

"What does that mean?"

"That means that no commitments are necessary. She's divorced, what used to be known as a 'woman of the world,' and I'm only one of several men she's seeing. We enjoy each other's company, and we're both adults."

"Do you see me as a *child?*"

"Don't be a fool! I see you as a beautiful and desirable woman. I've just told you so."

Before she knew what was happening, he was kissing her again, gently but skillfully, murmuring as his lips touched her eyes, her lips, her ears, the nape of her neck, the cleavage at the *V* of her dress.

"Then why treat me as a child?" she said, extricating herself from his embrace with an effort.

He had no answer, so she continued. "I'm perfectly able to take care of myself, make my own decisions, my own choices. You have no right to try to control everything. Don't you see how that turns it all into some kind of elaborate game? Why don't you just give us both a chance to explore whatever there is between us?"

"Do you think I don't want to?" His voice was bitter, and he began to pace restlessly. "You make it all sound so simple. It isn't. There's a great deal you don't understand—a great deal you don't know."

"Then suppose you begin by explaining it to me."

"I'm not sure that I can—that I have the right to."

"I don't understand why it has to be so difficult," Connie said, finally out of patience. "We're just going round and round in circles."

"That's what I mean. There's a lot you don't understand."

They looked at each other, pain and regret clear in Connie's eyes, a glacial imperiousness in his. Connie was the first to move. Overcome by a sense of futility, she turned away from him and headed blindly toward the door, only to collide with Martine, Janine—and the handsome stranger from the café in the Cours Mira-beau.

"Why, it's *la belle Americaine!*" he exclaimed with pleasure. Stunned for a moment, Connie quickly recovered and said, happy for the distraction, "Why it's Monsieur *Calisson et Pastis!* We seem destined to meet, don't we?"

"That's because the world is very small for those who love as we do," he said melodramatically, and with a cavalier flourish removed an imaginary plumed hat and made a sweeping bow.

Connie, aware of George's silent, brooding presence, deliberately played up to the Frenchman's playfulness.

"You two know each other?" Martine asked, caught short for once.

"Of course. We've shared a magic moment, haven't we, *ma belle?* And food and drink. I can never forget it—or your magnificent violet eyes," he concluded, his own blue eyes sparkling flirtatiously. "As a matter of fact, I know everything about you," he said, "except your name."

"It's Connie Wyatt," she said, extending a hand, which he gallantly kissed.

"Michel Chevigny, at your service."

"How amazing, George." Martine's bantering tone seemed a camouflage. "Here Connie's been hidden away in the country in a tiny school in Aix for just a little more than a week, and yet she has already managed to meet one of the most attractive men in France, a star of French cinema!"

No wonder he looked familiar, Connie thought.

"Our Connie is obviously a woman to watch." There was an edge of malice now in Martine's voice.

For a moment a storm of emotions passed over George's face—anger, jealousy, suspicion; then they were replaced by an icy impassivity.

"So it would seem," he said with cold affability. "So it would seem."

# Chapter Eight

"Miss Wyatt! Come downstairs right away! You'll never guess what's here for you!"

The unholy trio, their voices joined in a somewhat shrill three-part harmony, were outside Connie's bedroom door. With the addition of Diana, they had become a more harmonious quartet and Connie's most faithful followers. In the past three weeks, Michel Chevigny's flamboyant pursuit of Connie had quite displaced their interest in George Trevelyan and Martine Alexandre. For one thing, Diana's father was now going back and forth between Paris and Aix, so there was less to observe; but far more significant, Connie was their own teacher, and what could be more exciting than watching her being courted by a famous movie star!

The arrival of a gift had become an eagerly awaited Saturday morning ritual. The first Saturday had seen the delivery of an enormous cardboard mockup of a bottle of *pastis* filled with *calissons,* which Connie had shared with the rest of the school. The accompanying note had said, "In rememberence of our first meeting and in the hope of many more—Monsieur *Calissons et Pastis.*"

The following week had been marked by the delivery of a beautifully appointed picnic hamper containing a terrine of pâté de campagne, a platter of cheeses, a bottle of chilled Veuve Cliquot champagne, and some baguettes. The note attached said, "A loaf of bread, a jug of wine, and some other delicacies to be shared with your most ardent admirer, who will pick you up at eleven." It was signed "Michel."

Obviously this week's gift had arrived.

"I'll be there in a few minutes, girls," Connie called gaily, and as their footsteps receded down the stairs, she returned to the examination of her "wardrobe."

Reaching into the armoire, she noticed the shell-pink confection she had so foolishly put on that first Saturday four weeks ago. The dress hadn't been right then, and it never would be right. It created an image she no longer wanted to project, what they had called at college "too s s and g"—too sweet, simple, and girlish —and she didn't feel like any of those things!

Connie frowned. There was nothing in the closet that she was really satisfied with. All her clothes were those she had worn in college. She had bought nothing for this trip, and now she was glad. Her tastes had changed; her sense of herself had grown surer. She was looking forward to buying some new things here in France—had been planning to for the past few weeks, but because of Michel, she had not yet had a free Saturday. However, he had called yesterday and said he wouldn't be able to meet her until evening, so she had arranged with Pervenche to catch the ten o'clock bus from Aix into Marseilles for a shopping expedition.

With a sigh, she compromised on the outfit that seemed least offensive: a simple navy t-shirt and a lavender and navy wraparound madras skirt. Slipping into a pair of low-heeled navy sandals, she grabbed her bag, closed the door behind her, and hurried downstairs.

None of the previous gifts had prepared her for the extravaganza that awaited: a rough straw basket filled to overflowing with a profusion of wildflowers. Attached to the basket was a multitude of colored helium balloons from which trailed ribbon streamers.

Most of the girls were clustered around, chattering excitedly. "There's a note inside, Miss Wyatt," said Mary Leigh Stanford conspiratorially. She hovered close by, as though hoping its contents would be shared with her.

"So there is, Mary Leigh," said Connie, opening it. *"A ce soir"* was all the note said.

"Is he coming to pick you up this morning, Miss Wyatt?" Alice Williams asked.

It had not escaped Connie's notice that all the girls managed to be on hand within minutes of Michel's arrivals. It was a little like having twenty younger sisters, she thought good-humoredly. But she didn't mind, and Michel, obviously delighted to exercise his charm on females no matter what their age, had never discouraged their attentions.

"Girls! Why are you loitering out here in the hall? We have five minutes before the chartered bus for Nice arrives. Please go collect your things."

As they obediently dispersed, Miss Levering said, turning to Connie, "I don't know what's gotten into those girls lately." Actually, her tone suggested that she had more than a suspicion of what it was. "And Connie, I think it would be a good idea to take that upstairs." She pointed to the basket distastefully. "It makes such a clutter."

"An awful clutter," said Jane Hardcastle, bending

over to pick up a bachelor button that had fallen to the floor and replacing it in the basket. She handled it as if it were something unpleasant.

"I'll take care of it in a little while," Connie replied casually as she moved toward the dining room.

A month ago, eager to win Miss Levering's approval, she would have rushed to remove the offending object. But she had long since come to the conclusion that nothing she could ever do would satisfy those two joyless creatures. Disapproval was a way of life for Miss Levering, and echoing Miss Levering was a way of life for Miss Hardcastle. Once Connie had recognized that, she realized that their carping was not personal and began to relax. In spite of the emotional upheavals of the month, due mostly to George Trevelyan, she felt herself stronger, more confident. There was no doubt of her success as a teacher—even Miss Levering had acknowledged as much. She was well liked by the girls and, what was most important, she was beginning to enjoy her life, thanks in no small part to Michel.

It still hurt to see George Trevelyan come down from Paris to visit Diana—and Martine—but she was almost too busy to brood. Admittedly Michel did not engender the same kind of feeling as George Trevelyan had, but this other kind of relationship was considerably more relaxing, since she wasn't the slightest bit in love with Michel and therefore felt much more in control.

It was flattering to have him dance total attendance on the weekends, and fun to have him mysteriously disappearing and reappearing during the week with very little advance notice. Last Monday night, for example, his white Mercedes had come rolling totally unexpectedly up the school drive at about nine o'clock in the evening, and he had honked his horn confidently under her window.

"Madame's car is waiting," he called up to her when she looked down to discover the cause of the racket.

Hoping to keep the disturbance to a minimum, she had called out that she would be right down. "Now what's all this about?" she laughed, running over to the car.

"Hop in! We're going for a drive. Unless, of course, you've a better offer for this evening? I shouldn't really presume on two weeks of intense adoration."

"Unfortunately, your presumption is justified. No better offer has come along," she said in mock despair.

"Come on, then—you're wasting time. Hop in, I say!" He opened the door on her side with a flourish.

They had no sooner passed out of sight of the school than Michel turned down a little country road and stopped the car. With a practiced move, he took her in his arms and began to kiss her, tenderly at first, then with mounting intensity. For one brief moment she returned his kiss avidly, but suddenly found her response was dying. It was as if she were outside herself, watching. She admired his expertise, but it was meaningless. With a fierce act of will, she forced herself not to think of those other kisses, those other arms, that other body against hers.

Michel seemed more startled than disappointed when she pushed him away. "I don't please you?"

"It's not that. It's just that I don't feel that way about you." Reluctant to hurt his feelings, she added, "At least not yet."

"Not yet?" He seemed genuinely amused. "You mean, I've been too fast, too French?"

"Perhaps," she replied evasively.

"Oh well," he answered, good-humoredly releasing her and putting the car into gear, "I shan't give up. We'll just try a slower tempo."

Connie wondered then if that would make any difference. She hadn't thought it would, and now, six days later, she still didn't think so.

"*Quel panache,* Connie!" cried Pervenche, looking up from her coffee.

"What do you mean?" Connie asked, baffled.

"The basket of flowers, of course. You must admit that only the French understand how to court a woman in style." Pervenche had obviously been smarting under the rain of anti-French remarks that had poured torrentially from Cynthia Levering ever since they had arrived in Aix.

"Perhaps. In any case, I've never had presents that were so imaginative or as much fun!"

"It must be very exciting! He's so good looking." Then, unable to contain herself, Pervenche asked impulsively, "You really like him, *n'est-ce pas?*"

"It would be hard not to, wouldn't it? He's loads of fun. And very uncomplicated." Even as she said it, Connie realized that she felt this way because she had so very little invested emotionally. "But much as I hate to disappoint you, Pervenche, we're really just friends."

"I don't think that's the way Monsieur Chevigny feels."

"Oh, I doubt if he takes anything very seriously." Glancing over at Martine's empty place, she said, "I see Martine's already eaten. She's not usually up before I am."

"Well, she said something about going off with Mr. Trevelyan this morning." There was an imperceptible pause to see if the news had any effect, but Connie had schooled herself not to react to any mention of George Trevelyan and Martine; she found she was almost successful.

"Only an outing with a man could get her up so early on a Saturday morning," Pervenche added cynically.

"Speaking of outings, Pervenche, I guess I'd better pass up a second cup of coffee if we're going to catch the ten o'clock bus, especially since I promised Cynthia Levering I'd remove that basket of flowers. She found it a public nuisance."

Her eyes met Pervenche's and they both started to laugh conspiratorially.

"All right, run along. You can pick me up when you're ready."

The sight of George Trevelyan standing in the hallway took Connie completely by surprise. His tall, lithe body was outlined against the bright light from the open doorway as he disdainfully surveyed the festooned basket of flowers.

"And what is *this* supposed to be?" he asked caustically.

"Miss Levering didn't seem to like it either. But I do," she said almost defiantly.

For the first time Connie found herself leading from a position of strength with George. After all, he had no way of knowing the extent of her relationship with Michel, and if he thought it was more than it was, so much the better. She was glad that she had not rushed to carry out Miss Levering's instructions. If she had, he would never have seen Michel's present to her, and she was delighted that he had. It was petty of her, but she didn't care.

"Excuse me." She picked up the basket with its bobbing colored balloons, aware as she did so that she might be cutting a faintly silly figure. "I've got to run along now. Pervenche and I are catching the ten o'clock bus to Marseilles." Her triumph had turned hollow and her earlier effervescence had gone quite flat—perhaps because George was just standing there, perfectly at ease, while she . . . What was it about that man? Except for their brief meeting in the garden, she had scarcely seen him in the past three weeks, yet as soon as they were together for a moment, his mere presence made everybody else seem second-best. The very sound of his voice had an immediate effect on her, an effect she was powerless to control.

"It so happens," he said, "that I'm taking Martine into Marseilles. I'd be glad to drop you off."

"That's very kind of you, but Pervenche and I have already made our plans, and I think we'll just stick with them. Thanks anyway." There was no way she was going to get into that car with Martine Alexandre and George Trevelyan, even if it meant crawling to Marseilles on her knees!

"Oh, George," Martine trilled as she swept into the hall. "What do you think of Michel's amusing gift? Really, Connie's turned him into an infatuated schoolboy. I've never seen him like this before."

She flashed a smile at Connie. "Actually, the two of you make a very nice couple." As she spoke, she linked her arm into George's.

Catching the note of condescension in Martine's voice, Connie made a supreme effort to suppress her rage. "Thank you, Martine," she said in a controlled voice, "I'm glad we meet with your approval." Fighting the urge to turn on her heels and run, she stood waiting for a response, thinking that actually Martine and George made a rather incongruous couple this morning. For the first time Connie was struck by something vaguely inappropriate about Martine's lacquered looks.

Her black and taupe art deco crêpe de chine print dress and high-heeled black lizard pumps made her look absurdly overdressed next to George, who was wearing a pair of chinos and a pale blue shirt open at the throat. It was hard to believe that they could be going to the same place. She was suddenly struck by George Trevelyan's expression; it reminded her of the first time she had seen him. The sense of barely restrained anger, of tightly coiled rage, was almost palpable.

"I think we had better get going, Martine," he said, not even bothering to say goodbye.

What had triggered this? His offer to drive her and Pervenche into Marseilles had been more than a polite gesture—he had really meant it—yet now he could hardly wait to see the last of her. As she watched them walk off, Connie found herself hoping that his surprising surliness was in some way connected to the mention of Michel.

Connie was not the only one to have observed the departure of George and Martine.

"Those two are birds of a feather," Pervenche said to her as the bus sped toward Marseilles.

"Do you really think so? It struck me this morning how different they were."

Pervenche cocked her head to one side and studied her friend. "On the surface yes, but underneath, they're both ruthless."

"I don't think you're being fair, Pervenche. He's not at all ruthless."

"Perhaps not," Pervenche relented, "but there's no doubt that he was a hard, cold man where his wife was concerned. Look at him. Three months in her grave and he's already found a replacement! Have you never noticed that those 'business trips' to Paris always coincide with the days Martine's away, taking her mysterious 'tante' to specialists?"

Connie had indeed noticed the coincidence, but had tried to ignore it. Still, almost despite herself, she was about to spring to his defense when Pervenche suddenly exclaimed, "Oh, Connie. *Ma pauvre petite*, I haven't understood at all! You're still fascinated by this man, aren't you?"

"I've seen sides of him that convince me he's not at all the way you make him seem." *I have confidence,* she remembered saying to him in Ed Hamilton's office.

"What do you mean?"

What did she mean? She answered carefully, trying to be accurate. She remembered the passion in him—as real as the arrogance, as real as the rage. "I can only tell you that he's far from cold and unfeeling. And if he seems hard, I think he has been badly hurt."

"That man? Hurt? Hurt by what? Surely not the loss of his wife."

"I don't know."

"Then how can you be so sure?"

"I've only my feelings to go by, but I trust them." As she said those words, she realized with a shock that they were true, had been from the beginning. *I have confidence.*

And despite all her disquieting experience with him, despite the way he turned her inside-out with his unreasonable behavior, she realized that was true.

"My poor child! You're in love with him, aren't you?" Before Connie could reply, Pervenche rushed on. "Always remember that a leopard can't change his sports."

Relieved at the escape this Periwinklism provided from the dangerous topic, Connie burst into a peal of delighted laughter. "Pervenche, you are precious," she said as the bus swung into the Marseilles terminal.

A few minutes later they found themselves amid the throngs streaming along the Canebière, the main street of Marseilles. Pervenche, thoroughly at home, led Connie up a side street and onto another avenue lined by shops. With the enthusiasm of a teenager she explained, "We're sure to find something here, and it will be much less expensive than anything in Aix would be."

"Do you want to do any shopping for yourself, Pervenche?"

"No—but I will have to leave you after lunch to visit my cousin." She paused. "And surely you must have noticed over the years, Connie, that I already have my clothes—I don't have to buy them!"

Connie was too embarrassed to reply, but Pervenche went on good-naturedly, "Don't be disturbed, Connie. I've known all along that my wardrobe is a joke at Whittier. But you see, when I was young I had no money, and then later on I realized that clothes wouldn't really change my life. And this way I never have any trouble deciding what to put on in the morning."

A wave of affection for this good-humored, self-effacing woman swept over Connie. "Oh, Pervenche, I'm so glad I've had a chance to get to have you as a friend this summer."

They smiled warmly at each other in complete understanding.

The next couple of hours were spent darting in and out of shops as Connie busily tried on clothes. When they finally settled down for lunch in a café on the Old Port, Connie's purchases piled on a chair beside them, both women were tired but triumphant.

"You, Pervenche," Connie turned to her companion, "get credit for the coup of the afternoon. That dress is a beauty."

"It looks perfect on you," said Pervenche with authority. She had proved a surprisingly sharp shopper. It was she who had found the little boutique that was selling Cacharels at a discount, and once inside it was she who had spotted the beautifully cut purple and lavender print dress as being almost made to order for Connie. "It brings out the color of your eyes, and though it's very simple, it's smart. You can wear it almost anywhere."

Connie had fallen in love with it, so she didn't need much persuading, and the dress was the first in a series of lucky finds: in short order Connie had bought a pleated white linen skirt, a navy linen blazer, a navy and white long-sleeved print blouse, and a pale blue and white checked short-sleeved shirt. Their foray had left her filled with the curious sense of exhilaration peculiar to a successful shopping trip.

"This is my treat, Pervenche," Connie said firmly, after they had both ordered green salads, omelettes and two glasses of chablis. As they waited to be served, Pervenche, elated at being back in her native land, eagerly gave Connie a brief but colorful rundown on everything in sight: the Old Port, with its launches plying the harbor; the fish stalls finishing up the morning's sales; and in the distance a view of what Pervenche told her was the Château d' If, where Dumas' fabled Count of Monte Cristo had been imprisoned.

At one point, as Connie interestedly studied the constantly shifting scene in front of them, she noticed a familiar face in the crowd—in fact, two familiar faces, George and Martine. To her great relief she could see Martine steering George into an elegant restaurant across the way. Good. There wasn't much chance of running into them then. But she was even more relieved to find that they had escaped her companion's notice. She was conscious that she had never answered Pervenche's question on the bus, and it was one she didn't want to answer. Perhaps one she couldn't answer.

As they lingered over their coffee, they were the

target of many vendors. Connie rejected a chance to buy African masks, turned away a dealer in Arab prayer rugs, waved off a peanut vendor—but finally succumbed to the blandishments of an outlandishly dressed little man in a fez who offered to read her palm.

After studying it intently for a moment, he intoned, "There is confusion in your life. I'm having trouble reading the signs."

"So am I," admitted Connie with a laugh, which he ignored.

"See these two lines? This one represents a dark stranger, moody and passionate, given to bursts of temper; this other one—" he pointed to a fainter line "—is a blond, filled with light, always eager to laugh."

Connie gasped. She had entered into this in a playful spirit, and now she was aghast at how close to the target he was.

"What else do you see?" she asked, leaning forward intently.

Before the man could reply, Pervenche began to laugh.

"Ah, ma chère, I'm surprised at you." She put a few coins into the man's hand and waved him away. "Don't you realize what he was doing?"

Baffled, Connie asked, "What?"

"Well, listen to the music."

"The music?" For the first time she became aware of a jukebox in the rear of the café playing an old Edith Piaf recording. Listening intently, Connie heard the story of a woman who had two men in her life, one a tempestuous dark-haired man, the other a carefree blond. "So that's it," she said with a wry smile. "He really had me fooled for a moment. In any case, Pervenche, there aren't two men in my life."

"So it's George Trevelyan." Pervenche seemed crestfallen. "I had hoped Michel might be the one . . . I

144

guess I'm just an incurable romantic." She sighed, then continued, "You know, Connie, the unattainable is not necessarily the most desirable. I could be wrong, of course, but it seems to me that love should be very easy and direct."

"I know that you care about me, Pervenche, and that you're trying to be helpful, but all I can say is that things aren't always that simple."

*"Hélas,"* Pervenche said, then diplomatically changed the subject. "By the way, Connie, I've been meaning to ask you—how are you coming along with your plans for the end-of-term celebration?"

"Fine. I'll be making assignments on Monday, and I have you down for reciting a La Fontaine fable, if that's okay with you."

*"Très bien.* It will make me feel like a schoolgirl again!"

"I've worked it out so all the girls have something to do—songs, folk dances, poems—you know. But the big surprise—" She paused dramatically.

"What?" said Pervenche, her face bright with curiosity.

"Well, at Martine's suggestion, Michel has agreed to do a scene with me from the Musset play you lent me. Remember? *No Trifling with Love."*

"Cynthia Levering won't care for that at all!"

"Won't care for what?"

"Won't care for having Michel Chevigny so closely connected with a school activity. Only this morning she said that actors are not to be trusted. 'They have no character. They're so used to being everybody that they end up by being nobody in particular.' " In a remarkable display of mimicry, Pervenche had caught Cynthia Levering's tone exactly, and Connie couldn't help laughing.

"And now, *ma chère,* thank you for the lunch, but I

really must run. I'll see you back at the school this evening."

Sitting alone and sipping the second cup of coffee she had ordered, Connie looked around her with pleasure, deciding that half of Marseilles must be down here lunching, drinking, and watching the other half promenading along the crowded sidewalks in front of them. When her eyes and ears tired of the sights and sounds, she had only to look past the crowd to the more tranquil vision of sailboats scudding across the bay under the brilliant blue sky. Idly she thought of how she would enjoy being out on a boat. Or better yet, swimming in some quiet sunlit cove off the coast—with George, she admitted, as unbidden the image came to her. Her eyes closed as she imagined the scene.

"Let's do it."

For a moment she was so sure the voice was part of her daydream that she was reluctant to open her eyes, but she sighed softly and briskly shook her head to break the spell.

His tall frame blocking out everything else, George Trevelyan was standing in front of her.

Confused by his sudden appearance, she could only stammer in bewilderment, "What . . . what do you mean?"

"Have you lost your faith in wavelengths?" he questioned, his voice low and suggestive, his eyes gleaming with amusement.

The words brought her back to Mt. Vernon Place, to that afternoon when she had tried to explain what she meant by a real connection between two people. Unfortunately, she knew now that it wasn't that simple.

"Yes, you've taught me better!" She couldn't help the note of accusation in her voice.

"Peace, Connie, peace!" He threw up his hands in

mock self-defense, then looked at her sharply and added, "I hope you didn't mean that. I won't be responsible for that, you know. I'd sooner never see you again."

"No," she whispered, appalled at the idea that she might indeed never see him again. "No. Not you. Just what you once called 'experience,' I guess . . ." Determined to get off this dangerous ground, she continued more lightly, "But don't change the subject. What did your wavelengths tell you?"

He studied her a moment, then evidently decided to accept her statement and pulled a chair close and sat down beside her. "You were looking out at the bay just as I started to come toward you. Then you closed your eyes. I preferred to think that it wasn't a response to my approach, so I deduced—perhaps because I was thinking the same thing—that you said to yourself, 'I'd love to be out on the water now.' Am I right?"

"Half right," she acknowledged. "I changed a preposition after that—'*in* the water.' "

"Wavelengths check out perfectly." He smiled. "So let's."

"No sooner thought than done," she said mockingly.

"Why not? Life is a race with time. Come. I know a place called Niolon, not a half hour's drive from here." He had taken her hand and was already standing, waiting for her to pick up the change the waiter had brought her.

"You can't be serious, George," she objected.

"That shows how little you know me," he said, and then fighting back a grin, he added, still holding onto her hand, "But you probably think you have some objections? No, don't answer. Let me guess. First," he said thoughtfully, "there's 'I don't have a suit.' Answer: there are plenty of shops in Niolon where you can buy one."

He raised one dark eyebrow as if to check on his accuracy, and at Connie's amused nod he continued, "Second, there's 'I've just had lunch and I'm too full to swim.' Answer: you won't be a half hour from now."

Again he paused for confirmation and again Connie smiled her agreement.

"Finally—" his voice turned hard "—finally, you've decided you'd rather be with Chevigny. And there is no answer to that."

Connie felt as if she had been slapped. What did Michel have to do with this? How could he read her mind about silly things like bathing suits and be so dense about her feelings?

"Better have those wavelengths checked out," she replied defiantly, freeing her hand from his. "And by the way, where's Martine?"

"I have no idea. She merely asked me to drive her into town this morning. We had lunch, and then she left." The topic didn't seem to interest him.

Meanwhile, as if there could be no question of her compliance, he had gathered up all her packages and, taking her hand again, pulled her to her feet and said, "Let's go. My car is right around the corner."

Despite her resolutions where George was concerned, Connie found it easier to follow her heart than her head and go along. And as it turned out, he was right. They were able to buy suits in Niolon, and the half hour trip along the rocky coast to the almost deserted cove was just long enough and hot enough to make the azure Mediterranean water even more inviting. For two hours they swam and frolicked and sunned, taking turns diving off a concrete pier, and Connie admired the ease with which he hoisted himself from the water and turned to pull her up after him in one smooth gesture. His body was as powerful and supple as she had known it would be, and each time he drew her up from the water he exacted a salty kiss—a toll imposed and paid with the same happy pleasure.

It was the first time they had been alone for any length of time, the first time they had shared any physical activity; in fact, impromptu though it may have been, it was really their first date.

On the way back, feeling totally content and relaxed, Connie quite naturally rested her head on George's shoulder; and as he maneuvered the car through the weekend traffic, he put a bronzed arm around her, leaned down, and gently brushed his lips against her hair.

There was no need for words, but just as Connie was thinking that everything was finally simple and uncomplicated, George said, "I'll drop you off so that you can change, and I'll pick you up at about seven for dinner."

Dinner! Connie sat up with a start, remembering that she had promised to go out with Michel that night. "Oh, George, I'm sorry but I just can't this evening."

"Why not?" His hand tensed on the wheel.

"I have a date with Michel."

"Break it." He removed his arm from her shoulder.

"I can't. I wouldn't do that."

"Is he that important to you?" The words snapped out like bullets.

"That's not the point. I wouldn't do that to anyone."

"You would in a flash, if I mattered to you." His jaw had hardened, his sensual mouth was a narrow line.

"That has nothing to do with it. You just don't want to understand!"

He bit back a reply and once more retreated into himself.

They rode the rest of the way back in an uncomfortable silence neither tried to break. Only when they arrived at the school did Connie make an attempt to retrieve the day. Getting out of the car, she turned and said, "George, I hate the way this has ended, because the afternoon was very special."

"It might have been," he answered shortly, and sped away.

# Chapter Nine

Michel was to pick her up at eight, but she was ready before then, and at a quarter to the hour a restless Connie descended to her favorite nook in the garden. In an attempt to bolster her sagging spirits, she had put on the new Cacharel dress, but it failed to improve her frame of mind, and she continued to brood about the events of the afternoon.

She couldn't understand why George had reacted so strongly to Michel. Twice within just a few hours he had seemed to assume that she and Michel were seriously involved. Couldn't he sense that Michel was of no importance to her? That the relationship was based on Michel's persistence rather than on her interest? That given the opportunity she would far rather have been seeing him, George?

"How is it going?"

It was Michel's voice on the other side of the hedge, and Connie was about to make her presence known when she heard another familiar voice answer.

"Well, I think things will improve if you can continue to keep my little rival occupied." Martine gave a silvery laugh. "With your help, I may be able to land my rich American! By the way, I hope you don't find the assignment too tedious."

"Oh, you know, for an old friend . . . Actually, I'm enjoying it. She's quite charming."

Connie realized that she shouldn't be listening, but she was glad she was.

"I've taken every opportunity to point out your little romance to George—to tell him that as an old friend of yours I can tell that you're quite serious, and that as a woman, I can tell that Connie is quite taken with you."

"Would that were so." Michel laughed. "I've been told to slow down to an American tempo!"

"Poor Michel," Martine purred, "what a new experience that must be for you."

Their voices receded as they headed back to the building.

So that was it, thought Connie. That explained a great deal. Martine was feeding George's jealousy, and Michel's courtship, unflattering as she had to admit the idea was, was merely part of Martine's plot.

Though she was furious, she was determined not to let Michel know that she was on to him until she had had the time to think the situation through. She was not so much hurt or surprised as appalled by the cynicism of Martine and Michel. No trifling with love indeed!

"I cannot tell you, Connie, how sorry I am that I made the mistake of turning this whole production over to you, and I certainly regret that I agreed to allow you and Monsieur Chevigny to do the scene from Musset. This whole thing has turned into a nightmare, pure and simple. The students are completely out of hand. I just found Mary Leigh Stanford painted up like a chorus girl, and I'm convinced it's all because of that French matinee idol!"

"Oh, I don't think it's so serious. After all, it's just a stage all girls go through." And then, as further reassurance—although she found she really didn't care —she added, "And in any case, it will all be over tomorrow."

"Not one moment too soon!" Cynthia Levering snapped irritably, and stalked off.

Alone again, Connie smiled to herself. Cynthia Levering's hair would have curled had she overheard some of the conversations among those girls! However diverse the Whittier students might be, they were united in their passionate adoration of that "French matinee idol," and Michel had done nothing to discourage them. There was something almost innocent about the openness with which he courted admiration.

But ever since she had overheard his conversation in the garden, it had become difficult for Connie to continue to see Michel as an egotistic but basically charming playboy. After the first shock had passed, she realized that what she had initially taken as a lighthearted game had its ugly side. While there had never been any possibility of falling in love with Michel, she had been manipulated by him, or rather by him acting under Martine's orders.

And Martine's ruse had evidently had more than a little success, for ever since their afternoon in Niolon, George had studiously avoided Connie. She had had only one opportunity to speak to him, and that had been more than a week ago. Walking up the Cours Mirabeau last Sunday, she had spotted him sitting alone at the Deux Garçons, staring fixedly in front of him. On an impulse she had gone up to him and said, "I'm reduced to offering a penny for your thoughts— the wavelengths are obviously jammed these days."

He had looked up and she could see a spontaneous flicker of pleasure, quickly replaced by an expression of almost exaggerated indifference. In barely civil tones he replied, "I wouldn't want to put you to the expense. I doubt if my thoughts would give you any pleasure."

She had waited for a moment to see if he would continue. When it became clear that he was going to remain obstinately silent, she turned and left.

Whatever Martine's game plan, Connie had decided on *her* next move: she would have things out with Michel when the right moment presented itself. In the meantime she had remained detached, even during the rehearsals that had so inflamed the students, and eventually her cool attitude had penetrated even Michel's magnificent ego.

"You don't take me seriously, *ma belle,*" he had complained petulantly one afternoon following a rehearsal.

His patience with the "slower tempo" he had agreed to had worn thin. Feminine resistance was new to this man who had been the beloved of some of the most beautiful women in France, and what had originally been a stimulating challenge was fast becoming a siege too prolonged for his tastes.

"Oh, no, Michel, you're wrong. I do take you seriously—particularly as an actor."

"What about as a man?"

Connie studied him quietly for a moment, then said deliberately, "What *am* I to think of you as a man, Michel?"

He was genuinely puzzled by her question. "I don't understand."

"Would it help if I told you that I know what you and Martine have been up to?"

He took a moment to absorb this, and Connie could all but hear the gears shifting. With a Gallic shrug and a boyish laugh, he said lightly, *"Touché."*

"Is that all you have to say?" She gasped at his effrontery. "You're really shameless, aren't you, Michel?"

"I rather thought of myself as loyal. After all, Martine is an old friend, and I saw no harm in helping her. She's tired of teaching, tired of living in Aix. Trevelyan seemed a possible way out."

"That was very noble of you, Michel," Connie said. "I hope that keeping me occupied wasn't too boring for you."

His bright blue eyes sparkled with indignation. "Far from it! You must not forget that my interest in you began long before Martine ever said anything to me. She merely encouraged what was a natural inclination. It seemed a happy coincidence to me. After all, how often can a man pursue what he wants and at the same time help out an old friend?"

In spite of herself, Connie admired his fancy footwork in a tight spot, and, as though sensing this, he pressed on. "In any case, it's not how we started but where we are going that counts." They were standing on the small bare stage, and now he moved closer and took her hands in his. "You know, Connie," he said, "I generally am aware when a woman finds me attractive, and I pride myself on never having forced myself on anyone. Yet you continue to rebuff me. Don't you like me?"

Freeing her hands, she answered, "It's what you've done that I don't like. Not only is it dishonest, but you've created a lot of complications in my life."

Abruptly, as if the possibility had just occurred to him for the first time, he asked, "Does that mean there's someone else?"

Her reluctance to reply was clue enough for him. "There is! Don't tell me you love George Trevelyan!"

Then, as if putting together all that he knew about the characters in this real-life drama, he exclaimed, "You do! I should have known! When Martine brought him in to watch us rehearse the other day, you suddenly turned to wood on that stage. I thought Martine was making you uncomfortable, but it was Trevelyan, wasn't it?"

His words brought back that moment when she had looked out and found George's eyes fixed on her. She knew he had finished his business in Paris and was spending this last week in Aix, but he had again avoided her; she certainly hadn't expected to have him watch her rehearse with Michel. Martine had been whispering into his ear, but he had seemed completely impervious to what she was saying, wholly concentrated on the love scene being played out before him. Just before it ended, he said something to Martine and left abruptly. If Connie had turned to wood, it was because she had been aware of no one else in that room but George Trevelyan.

"It *is* Trevelyan, isn't it?"

Connie maintained her obstinate silence.

"You don't have to answer. Your face has told me everything. Ah, well." He grinned mischievously. "I refuse to give up."

That had been only a few days ago, and since that time Michel had redoubled his efforts. Tonight he had arranged for the four of them to go to a performance of Mozart's *Don Giovanni* in the courtyard of the Archbishop's Palace, next to the cathedral of St. Saveur. Martine had not been particularly happy when Michel had arrived, tickets in hand, but he had insisted that they go. Getting four seats at the last minute had been quite a coup—even for Michel—but more to the point, he was eager to take the measure of his rival at close quarters. If Michel had started out in the service of Martine, he was now acting solely in his own behalf, and he seemed to have no doubts of his ultimate success.

Connie, on the other hand, was uneasy about the evening. Much as she would have liked to be able to deal directly with the intrigue that Martine had concocted, there was no way she could expose her without in some way making a fool of herself. She could hardly indicate to George that Martine had her eye on him and was so bent on getting what she wanted that she had even drawn Michel into her plot. She was afraid that these maneuvers, once revealed, would inflame George. Remembering as she did his barely contained anger in the Lexington Market, she shuddered to think how he might react. Instinctively she knew that once unleashed, his fury would be uncontrollable, and she found the idea frightening.

"Once there, you'll give me your hand, and you'll say yes," sang Don Giovanni, and, as though on cue, Michel reached over and took Connie's hand in his. The gesture was not lost on George Trevelyan, who was seated on her left, next to Martine. Seeing this, Connie, who had been about to withdraw her hand, decided not to. The game would have to go on a little longer.

The only trouble was that the game was getting rougher.

*"Don Giovanni* is my favorite opera," said Michel during the intermission.

"It would be," Martine snapped. "It must be like seeing your own life set to music."

Relations between the two had become somewhat strained. Connie wondered if George was aware of it too.

"Retract your claws, my love," Michel retorted. "You weren't always that unhappy with your Don Giovanni!"

Martine's angry look provided Connie with the final confirmation of what she had recently begun to suspect —Michel and Martine had been lovers, and, for all she knew, perhaps still were. A lot of things suddenly fell into place. That very first day on the Cours Mirabeau, Michel had raced off because he was late for a rendez-vous, and later that evening she had found Martine in a foul mood, grumbling about men who never turn up when they say they will. Could the rendezvous Michel was late for have been with Martine? And those convenient illnesses of Martine's famous *tante*—they coincided not only with George's trips to Paris, as Pervenche had pointed out, but with Michel's mysterious absences from Aix. Perhaps George had never been involved with Martine; perhaps, like Pervenche, she had "jumped over conclusions."

"He amuses you?" asked Martine, seeing the sudden smile on Connie's face and completely misinterpreting it.

"Amuses and instructs," she replied cryptically.

"Instructs. In what way?" George handed Martine the glass of champagne for which she had sent him and turned to Connie. His voice expressed a kind of tolerant contempt; it said as clearly as words that he thought it highly unlikely that Michel could instruct anyone in anything.

Connie wondered if she could be imagining it, but it did seem to her that George was more relaxed about Michel.

"Come now, George, don't be naïve," Martine said knowingly.

The silence that greeted this comment made it clear that her effort to create an air of intimate complicity with George had failed, and with a falsely bright smile she turned to Connie and, taking in the Cacharel, said, "How nice to see you in a becoming dress."

Connie was glad she had decided to wear it. Michel, of course, had seen the dress before, but that made no difference. George had never seen her in it, and she hadn't needed Martine's double-edged comment to assure her of how well she had chosen. The small violet flowers of the dress brought out the full beauty of her long-lashed violet eyes, and its simple cut and supple fabric emphasized her firm, full breasts and small waist. Even among the glittering crowd of the famous and near-famous that had turned out for this performance, her fresh beauty had attracted admiring glances.

"I'm glad you like it," Connie answered, deciding to reply only to Martine's words rather than their intent.

"There are definite advantages to buying one's clothes in France."

"Not necessarily," Connie replied sharply, taking in Martine's costume for the evening—a black chiffon that succeeded in revealing everything it purported to cover. It was a dress that left nothing to the imagination, and it was, Connie decided, a measure of Martine's desperation. There was no doubt that it drew interested glances from all the men, but it was a kind of attention Connie would not have wanted.

The sparring between the two women had not escaped Michel's notice, and his glance went delightedly from one to the other. George, however, remained impassive, aloof, almost distracted—although from time to time Connie felt his eyes on her.

Martine's return shot, if indeed she had one, was blocked by the warning bell for the next act of the opera.

*"Dommage,"* said Michel as they went back to their seats.

159

"What's too bad?" asked Connie.

"I liked the dialogue. That was a good scene you two were playing."

The bloodletting had released some of Connie's tension, and during the rest of the performance she found herself thoroughly swept up in the engulfing crescendo of music. When Don Giovanni had been pulled down to hell and the curtain had descended amid thunderous applause, she turned instinctively to George, who had already turned to her. They were both too moved to speak. Only their eyes communicated, but it was enough. It was as if they were again one, in total understanding. They were reluctant to leave behind not only the impact of the music but, more important, the connection that had once more been forged between them. Connie was sure that she and George could have instantly cleared up all the misunderstandings between them had it not been for the presence of Martine and Michel. But they were very much there, and even now Michel had taken her arm possessively and was steering her through the crowds outside the Archbishop's Palace. Looking back at George regretfully, Connie saw that Martine had him firmly in tow.

"I wish we could shake those two," Michel murmured. "Your friend Trevelyan has a certain power, but he's as dreary as an undertaker—and Martine's not much better." There was a tinge of respect in his voice as he added, "I must say, there aren't many men who can say no to Martine when she sets her mind on something."

Connie said nothing; she was quite sure that George would say yes or no only according to his wishes—not anyone else's. As they stopped on a corner to wait for George and Martine to catch up she compared both men: Michel, a laughing blond grownup child in a high-fashion white silk suit, a dark blue and white foulard dramatically tucked into the collar of his shirt, and George, darkly handsome and quietly but undeniably masculine in his less spectacular but impeccably tailored blue blazer and white flannel trousers. It occurred to her that Michel would look much better with Martine, and she wished with all her heart that it were in her power to pair them off.

No sooner had George and Martine made their way through the crowds to join them than Michel quickly seized the lead. "It's stifling here, and anyway everything's going to be packed. Why don't we just get into my car and out of town?"

Connie quickly rejected the idea. "Oh, Michel, if you don't mind, I'd much rather take a final look at Aix at night. This is my last weekend here, you know." While that was what she preferred, it was really that she didn't want to be paired off with Michel on a dance floor—or worse, have to watch Martine in George's arms.

"I'd prefer that too," George said decisively.

Martine made a moue of disappointment and was about to protest, when George, seeing her reaction, forestalled her objection by adding, just as calmly as before, but in a tone that suggested it would not be wise to argue, "You and Michel will have many opportunities to go dancing, Martine, so you must allow Connie and me our way this evening."

Connie's heart leaped. In linking her name with his, George had not only in some way publicly uncoupled himself from Martine, but had seemed to imply some kind of parallel life with Connie—as if "they" might not have the chance to see Aix again, and conversely as if wherever he went, she too might be going.

"In that case," Michel said, reading the determination behind the bland statement and choosing to give in gracefully, "I will be your guide." It was the only way left to him to control the situation.

"Lead on, Chevigny." George's voice suggested that he was prepared for the moment to tolerate Michel. Connie looked up at George at that moment, and she could have sworn that he winked at her conspiratorially.

As they walked slowly through the gracious old town, pausing at some of the illuminated churches, stopping to admire once more the famous old clock tower, savoring the sudden unexpected view of quiet private courtyards along the silent side streets, there was an unavoidable shifting and reshifting of couples. At one point Connie and George found themselves alone.

"Isn't it beautiful," she said softly.

"*You're* beautiful, Connie, and you make everything else seem so too." His low voice stirred her as it always did.

"How do you do it?"

"Do what?" she asked, trembling at the sensation of his warm breath at her ear as he lowered his head to hers.

"Always look better than I remember. That's been true, you know, from the very first." He paused, then said almost as if to himself, "I never thought when we met in Baltimore that we'd be sharing a night like this. Yet it seems very natural, very right, doesn't it?"

Suddenly Connie heard Pervenche saying, "Love should be very easy and direct." She could hardly say that those words described the course of her relationship with George Trevelyan up to now, but there was something different about him tonight; it was as if he had come to some conclusion, disposed of some problem. Mozart's magic music had made a path for them through the maze of their complicated emotions. Something had also happened to dispel whatever notions he had had about the role Michel played in her life. If she had begun to suspect that Martine was not important to him, perhaps he had discovered that Michel was equally unimportant to her.

There was a flicker of annoyance in George's face as Martine and Michel rounded a corner and came into sight again. "I wish we could get rid of those two!" he exclaimed impatiently, unknowingly echoing Michel. "It's you I want to be with." His eyes flashed and he added rapidly, "Say the word and I'll manage something!"

Connie shook her head regretfully. "No, we can't."

"I knew you'd say that." He looked at her ruefully and said, half humorously, half sardonically, "Remember the prince with the perfect pitch? This claimant has hit a few wrong keys, hasn't he?"

"You remember that?"

His eyes held hers. "I remember every word of every conversation we've ever had. I remember the touch of your lips, the feel of your—"

"Do you hear that, Connie?" Michel's voice broke in excitedly.

Connie had heard nothing but George, could still hear nothing but the echo of his voice.

Impatiently Michel persisted. "Don't you hear that music, Connie? That's the real thing—an old-fashioned accordionist—and I can tell from here that he's very good. You must listen and dance, or you will have missed a bit of old France!" He seized her wrist and pulled her along, calling exuberantly over his shoulder, "We're going dancing. Don't just stand there, come on!"

Martine, who had obviously been bored by the tour of Aix, which she knew only too well, brightened visibly. "The gods are merciful," she said, turning to George. "I'd given up all hope of dancing tonight."

Connie knew the interruption didn't matter. There had been a turning point. From here on in, she felt in her heart that there could no longer be any significant rupture between them.

The music turned out to be coming from a small café, which on this festival night had become an impromptu *bal musette*. Every table was filled, the crowd a mix of elegant international jetsetters, casually dressed students, and local townspeople. Inside, the accordionist had set himself up at the rear of the café, where tables had been cleared away to make room for a handkerchief-sized dance floor. As the four of them stood watching from the entrance, the *patron*, who obviously had more than a nodding acquaintance with Michel and Martine, rushed over and greeted them warmly.

"How nice to see you two again. You haven't been here in quite a while. Ah, you were at the opera tonight!" he exclaimed, seeing the program in Michel's pocket. "Tell me, is that new soprano as good as they say?" And with the passion of a true opera lover, he began to bombard them with questions about the performance.

Seeing the two temporarily entangled, George took advantage of the opportunity and, turning to Connie, said, "I've never danced with you before." His gaze seemed to engulf her and she felt a mounting excitement.

"That can easily be remedied," Connie replied just as Michel came hurrying over.

"Ah, no, Trevelyan. I'm afraid the first dance is mine. Why don't you go rescue Martine from that opera-maddened bore."

Ignoring Michel, George turned and looked at Connie questioningly.

"I really think you owe it to Martine to rescue her,"

she said tremulously, "but I hope you'll claim the next one."

To her vast relief, he smiled into her eyes and said approvingly, "On consideration, I do believe I like your sense of honor." And after an ironic bow to Michel, he walked back to Martine.

A murmur of recognition swept over the other dancers as Michel guided Connie onto the tiny dance floor. No sooner had the two of them begun to dance than the other couples glided away, retreating to the sidelines to watch. Much as Connie enjoyed Michel's expertise, she nonetheless wished it were George's arms that were around her.

It was a bravura performance, the accordionist goading Michel to meet the pace, inspiring Connie to match his every move. Several times it seemed the dance was about to end, but as if reluctant to give up the spotlight he shared with the famous movie star, the accordionist segued from one melody into another without pause.

Finally, as the music reached a dramatic finale, Michel bent Connie back with a flourish into a dramatic dip. Then, smoothly raising her to him, kissed her full on the lips. The crowd went wild.

Exhilarated by the attention, Michel generously surrendered Connie to George, and, turning to Martine, announced, as if distributing favors, "Now it's your turn!" As he led Martine back to the dance floor, once again crowded with other couples, Connie turned expectantly to George. Given his previous good-humored acceptance of the situation, she was ill prepared for the look that greeted her.

"George, what's the matter?"

She was frightened. He seemed so far away, his eyes focused on some inner vision.

"George!" she repeated. "What is it?"

"She was like that too."

"Who was?"

"Amanda."

"What do you mean?"

"Like you just now."

"I don't understand."

The music reached a climax and suddenly stopped, so that even though George had not been speaking very loudly, his words were distinct and could be heard by everyone around them.

"Like you just now. Any man would do. All she needed was a pair of arms around her—it never mattered whose." As Connie looked at him in stunned disbelief, he turned away abruptly and stalked out of the café.

# *Chapter Ten*

"I thought Americans were supposed to be such good sports. All I can see is a sore loser."

Michel's mood was reflected in his petulant tone as he drove Connie and Martine back to the school where both had insisted on being taken shortly after George Trevelyan had rushed out of the café. The fact that he suddenly had Martine on his hands had dampened Michel's plans for the evening, and he was furious at the curtailment of his own pleasure.

"I don't know what you mean," Connie said defensively.

"When your George Trevelyan saw he couldn't meet the competition, he behaved like a spoiled child and just walked out."

"Oh, do be quiet, Michel!" Martine was curled in the back seat, a look of discontent on her face. "You're so hopelessly vain. Why do you automatically assume that people are competing with you?" Indifferent to Connie's presence, she went on, "You know, I'm beginning to think you're a bit stupid as well. You're always saying that Americans are simple souls, easy to handle, but that's certainly not been my experience. If George Trevelyan were a spoiled child, Michel, I'd have had no trouble with him. After all," she concluded angrily, "I've had enough practice with you!"

Connie hoped that their private argument, now escalated to a full-blown fight, would keep the conversation from returning to George. When Martine and Michel had come back from their dance, they had been surprised to find her standing alone; she had been unable to give an explanation for George's departure then, nor could she come to his defense now.

Mercifully the ride back was short. As soon as the car stopped in the driveway, Martine stormed out, slamming the door behind her in a surge of anger and frustration.

As Connie started to get out too, Michel reached across her and grabbed the handle of the door. "No, no," he said, apparently not even flustered by the angry exchange of the previous five minutes, "the night's just beginning for *us*."

Connie found it hard to believe that anyone could be so onstage all the time, and she replied with impatience, "I'm afraid not, Michel. I'm very tired and I have a lot to do tomorrow." Firmly she removed his arm and slid from the car before he could even attempt to kiss her good night, adding more kindly once she was out, "Thanks for everything, Michel. I loved the opera —and you *are* a wonderful dancer."

"*Bon*." His good humor had returned, and he added seductively, "Don't think you will get away from me so easily tomorrow. We won't let the others interfere again." As he drove back down the drive he suddenly began honking the horn exuberantly, as though in celebration. Obviously he had understood nothing.

Afraid she would be unable to fall asleep, Connie stood for a long time on her little balcony. Though the garden below was now a familiar part of her life, its beauty—night or day—never failed to delight and soothe her. When she finally went to bed, she fell into a dreamless sleep as soon as her head hit the pillow.

Up early, her first waking thought was of George Trevelyan. There had to be some explanation for his behavior. It couldn't be jealousy—whatever he may have thought at first, he had certainly understood by the time they left the opera that there was nothing serious between her and Michel, and he had even approved of her decision to give Michel the first dance.

Last night was the first time George had ever mentioned his dead wife's name: perhaps Amanda was the key to it all. What had that beautiful woman she had seen him with last year at the symphony really been like? All Baltimore had seen her as a victim of his jealous rages, but was that the truth?

Connie longed to see George and talk to him. She frowned as she realized that she might not have the opportunity until evening, if then. The performance and the party afterward would hardly provide many opportunities for a quiet private talk.

The problem was in the forefront of her mind as she rapidly buttoned the blue and white striped searsucker sundress she wore on particularly hot days. This one, she realized as she came down the stairs, was going to be a scorcher.

"Oh, good, there you are, Connie." Pervenche was standing guard over a long narrow wicker basket. "The girls," she said in an attempt to disguise her own excitement, "can hardly wait to see what Michel has sent this week."

The game had ceased to amuse Connie, and she found she had little interest in Michel's latest offering. "Why not open it and see, Pervenche?" she said indifferently.

The dozen long-stemmed red roses inside the covered basket, though lovely, were an anticlimax from the girls' point of view, accustomed as they were to something more flamboyant, and they scattered moments later, their curiosity satisfied.

Only Pervenche's enthusiasm remained unchanged. "Read the card, Connie," she said, eagerly plucking it from among the roses, which were already filling the entrance hall with their scent.

Connie obediently reached out for the card. A moment later her face was radiant.

"Oh, Pervenche, I'm so happy. He'll be here soon!" Impulsively she extended the card to Pervenche.

My apologies for last night. Will you spare me some time this morning? I'll pick you up at ten. Please.
George

Pervenche looked up, stricken, and sighed. "I can see that George Trevelyan is the one who really matters to you. None of Michel's gifts made you look like this."

Connie gave a happy laugh. "You needn't sound so gloomy about it, Pervenche!"

"I'm not convinced that there's anything to rejoice over." She sounded troubled. "Don't forget, *ma chère,* he's so much older than you."

"Oh, Pervenche, don't be silly! After all, he's only thirty-seven. That's not much older than Michel, and you were never bothered about *his* age!"

Pervenche paused to consider this. "That's true," she admitted, "but perhaps it's not so much the number of years, but what those years have done to one."

"Those years have made him what he is. And I know now that what he is is what I want."

Connie's voice carried so much conviction that Pervenche's objections were stilled.

"You're right not to listen to me, my child." Pervenche gave her a hug. "One must do what one must do."

"Connie!" Cynthia Levering's voice was sharp. "Have you had breakfast yet?"

"No, Miss Levering. I may just have a cup of coffee before I go out."

"Go out? What do you mean? Wherever are you going? There's a great deal to do here today."

"I've already taken care of everything that can be done now. Anyway, I'll be back around lunchtime."

This was said with such firmness that Cynthia Levering was forced to recognize that she was now dealing with a very determined young woman.

"Very well, but be sure that you are." And having had her usual final say, she hurried off.

Connie had hardly heard her. "Oh, Pervenche, he'll be here any minute. I think I'd just as soon meet him by the gate."

It was, she realized, her earlier fantasy come true, though with some major differences.

Selecting one of the roses from the basket, she broke off the stem, tucked the flower into the low-cut bodice of her dress, and ran out the door.

As she hurried past the garden to the gate, she was stopped by Diana. "Are you meeting Monsieur Chevigny?"

Connie paused for a moment, then, studying the girl closely, said, "No, as a matter of fact, I'm meeting your father. He's going to pick me up in a few minutes."

"I'm so glad, Miss Wyatt!" She started to say something else, but then stopped.

"What is it, Diana?" Connie asked gently.

"I just wanted to tell you that Mary Leigh invited me to go along with her family to Italy for two weeks, and my father said it's all right. The Stanfords are coming tomorrow morning, and we'll be leaving after lunch. Isn't that great?"

"How nice for you." Connie hugged Diana impulsively.

"I'm glad it's my father you're seeing this morning," Diana blurted out.

"So am I," Connie replied honestly.

Smiling, she continued down the drive and reached the gate just as George drove up. He leaned over to open the door for her. "I wasn't sure you would agree to see me after last night." His voice was grave, and his eyes searched her face, traveled down to where the rose lay, then up again.

"After last night it was all the more important that I see you again."

"Yes, I know." All trace of arrogance was gone. "I owe you an explanation. Not only for last night, but for everything. I once said that there were things I had no right to tell you. I was wrong." A quick smile passed over his face. "I've often been wrong where you're concerned, haven't I, Connie?" He didn't wait for an answer. "Anyway, I've decided I have no right *not* to explain them. Come on, get in. We'll go somewhere where we can talk."

They drove along in silence, Connie content to wait, George driving quickly and surely along back roads to what was clearly a specific destination.

"Here we are," he said at last as he parked the car on the side of the road. He turned to her. "Let's get out and walk a while."

They were on a high rise of land overlooking a medieval town nestled into the side of a cliff. It was like a fairy-tale illustration, but neither of them was in the mood to appreciate it, and without even exchanging a word, they headed toward a small, cool-looking glade.

172

As they neared it, Connie could hear the ripple of water—an unusual sound in Provence, as she had discovered this summer.

"This is beautiful," she said, turning to George. "How did you find it?"

"It's one of my favorite places. I've come here often."

"With Martine?" She bit her lip. "I'm sorry. I have no right to ask that."

He shook his head impatiently. "You have every right to ask."

She remained silent; it was George who had to speak.

"Make yourself comfortable," he said finally. "I have a lot to say."

He waited while she settled, tucked her feet under her, and leaned back against the low natural rise. Only then did he sit down too.

As she waited for him to speak, she studied his face, that face that had become so familiar to her during the past two months. She had seen him enraged, bitter, withdrawn—and sympathetic, passionate, happy; but behind each of those façades had always been a man of impenetrable mystery. Now his gray eyes met hers in perfect candor.

"Let's dispense with the least important thing first," he said dryly. "I have never been here with Martine. Despite what you may think, there is nothing between Martine and me, there never has been."

"Is that the way she sees it?"

He considered the question for a moment and then answered, "Perhaps not. I've always been quite aware of Martine's opportunistic side—though I must admit I didn't figure out what game she and Michel were playing till a few days ago—and I can only tell you that for my part there has been nothing between us, nor have I ever given her any reason to think that there would be." He made an impatient gesture. "But that's not what I want to talk to you about. Martine and Michel aren't important—*we* are. I guess I'd better begin with last night."

"Yes," Connie said levelly, "I was completely confused. If you understood that Michel wasn't important to me, what did I do to make you so angry?"

He reached for her hand and kissed it lingeringly. *"You* did nothing. But the situation reminded me . . ."

". . . of Amanda?"

Deliberately he released her hand, and his eyes locked with hers. "Look, Connie, let me do this my way. Bear with me, will you?" He laughed mirthlessly as he added, "You've had to do a lot of that, I know, but you've got to realize that this isn't easy for me. I've never spoken to anyone about Amanda. But you must know the truth about her before you can understand anything about me."

His jaw was set with determination, and Connie could see that whatever he was going to say caused him great difficulty.

"Amanda was not made for marriage. She liked men too much to be able to confine herself to only one." Whatever he had once felt, his voice was now deliberately matter-of-fact. "Unfortunately, I didn't discover this until after Diana was born. At first I hoped we could work it out, that having a child to raise would help. And I thought it was in some way tied to her drinking. But even when she stopped drinking—and she would, from time to time, if only because she thought it was hurting her looks—the affairs went on."

His eyes had never left Connie's face, and, reading the surprise there, he asked, "Are you shocked?"

"Not shocked. Just amazed at how little you can tell

from appearances. You know, I saw the two of you together at last year's symphony benefit, and I thought you made such a wonderful couple."

He laughed bitterly. "Yes, so much for appearances. I remember that night very well. We had had a terrible scene, and I had asked her again to give me a divorce. I would have made it well worth her while."

"And she wouldn't?" Connie asked.

"She told me again she would never give up being Mrs. George Trevelyan. She liked her life as it was." His eyes were cold. "It was my fault, too, Connie. I was blinded by her beauty when I married her. I had no idea of how calculating she was, no idea of what she was really like."

"But if what you say is true, surely you must have had grounds for divorcing her."

"Not without creating a scandal that would have hurt Diana, and I would never do that. Oh, there was no way to keep the drinking hidden from Diana, and unfortunately she's known for a long time that her mother had as little genuine affection for her as she did for me. But she's still a child, and luckily she didn't understand that her mother was a wh—" His voice had become increasingly harsh. He broke off abruptly, then continued in a more controlled tone. "Let's just say that she had no way of understanding her mother's true nature. And I wanted to keep it that way as long as I could."

"How hard that must have been for you," she murmured. "And how unfair!" she added indignantly.

"The gossip, you mean?"

Before Connie could reply, he continued, "I know about it, Connie. Even some of my oldest friends believed it." There was a brief pause, then he added acidly, "I'm supposed to have made my beautiful wife's life a living hell by never letting her out of my sight, by flying into jealous rages. Well, the truth is I'd ceased to care about the lovers—it had been a long time since we had lived together as man and wife—but I let people think what they would. The important thing was to keep Diana from finding out. I didn't love Amanda, but I did try to keep an eye on her. I insisted she be discreet about her affairs, and I watched her drinking like a hawk. When she got drunk, she was a danger to herself and everybody around her. The fire . . ." For a moment he looked beyond Connie, at some private hell.

"Are you sure you want to talk about it, George?"

"Of course I don't want to talk about it!" he snapped. Then, more gently, "I'm sorry, Connie. I didn't mean to lose my temper. I want you to know everything. I want no secrets between us." He cupped her chin and made her eyes meet his gaze. "That's what you want, too, isn't it?"

She nodded, and he removed his hand and continued.

"The night of the fire I had no idea Amanda was in the house. She'd said she was going to visit friends in Washington. I knew what that meant, of course—she was going off with her latest lover—but I'd long before stopped challenging those lies. The fire started in the early hours of the morning. It woke me up. I got Diana out as quickly as I could, and we stood on the lawn, watching the house go up in flames. The first I knew about Amanda's being inside was when the fire chief came up and told me they had found a body in the study on the first floor, which was where the fire had started. I can only suppose that she and her lover had had a fight and that she came home during the night without my being aware of it, drunk as usual. She must have been smoking when she passed out on the couch."

He seemed so far away, so isolated in his revived anguish, that Connie instinctively reached out and touched his hand. "What a terrible experience! And how awful all those years must have been!"

"Oh, you needn't feel sorry for me," he said curtly. "You can learn to adjust to almost anything. I won't say that I lived the life of a saint, but I did manage to live without the complications of love. At least until I met you. Then, despite all my resolutions . . ."

Connie was almost embarrassed at her own joy. "Are you saying that you love me, George?" Her voice was almost a whisper.

"Isn't that obvious?" He smiled at her, though he seemed genuinely surprised at the question.

"Not exactly. It hasn't been that easy to read you."

"I suppose not," he agreed finally. "I've been denying my feelings all along. How could you have known when I wouldn't let myself know?"

"That first day . . ." Connie began hesitantly.

"That first day I fell in love with the way you *looked* in the Market, and I fell in love with what you *are* in Ed's office." There was no hesitation or uncertainty in his words. He looked almost exultant at finally saying them.

"Then why did you leave me like that in Mt. Vernon Place?"

"It was so complicated! How can I make you understand? Just being with you, talking to you, was so wonderful—for the first time in years I felt connected with someone. And then something you said made me realize how young you were, and I felt I had to pull away while I still could."

"At the time I couldn't figure out *what* had happened. Later I thought that might be it, but it seemed so silly!"

"It isn't all that silly, Connie. Not even now. But then—oh, it just seemed all wrong to let you get involved."

"Wrong to let *me* get involved—or you, George?"

"So you *have* understood me, Connie! Yes, that's exactly what I've been trying to explain. I liked to think that I was trying to protect you, but I know now I was really protecting myself. I didn't want to be in love, so I wouldn't let it happen."

"And since then?"

"Since then that same self-protection has colored everything that's happened between us. Ever since that day in Baltimore I hadn't been able to get you out of my mind. When you called me in Paris, just the sound of your voice was incredibly exciting, and when I saw you again in Aix I realized I wanted you more than I had imagined it possible to want any woman. But all that feeling frightened me. I didn't know how to handle it, so I tried desperately to convince myself that I could get it out of my system by just having an affair with you."

"Then why . . . I mean . . . that night in my room . . ."

"I walked away from you, Connie, but not because the time and the place were inappropriate." His eyes were warm and his voice caressed her, though he otherwise deliberately kept his distance. "Connie, my love, do you really think that in one more minute either of us would have cared about that?"

Connie could feel herself blushing.

"Don't be embarrassed, my darling. I love your passion, just as I love everything else about you. But I walked away for the same reasons I walked away in Baltimore. I couldn't admit to myself that I loved you, and though I tried I found I couldn't offer you less than love."

"Is that why you stayed away?"

He corrected her. "That's why I *tried* to stay away. I didn't seem to be able to manage it, though. I fought against seeing you because when I did I forgot everything but how much I wanted you—and that was dangerous."

"But there was one point," she said, determined to understand everything, "when you didn't try to see me at all."

"Don't remind me of that!"

"No, please, George. I want to know."

"You want me to grovel? To confess that I really thought you were interested in Michel? All right," he said bitterly, "I admit it. I kept hearing about how often you went out with him, and I felt that since I wasn't prepared to claim you, the least I could do was leave Chevigny à clear field."

"But George, I never loved Michel! I—"

"I know, Connie. I realized that when I finally brought myself to watch a rehearsal. I still didn't dare hope that you loved me, but I could see that you didn't love him. And I could see a lot of other things too, but there was no point in blaming Martine. It was my fault because I had been fighting so hard to avoid admitting how much I loved you."

Connie finally broke the silence that followed.

"And now that you know that you do love me?" She forced herself to be still.

"Ah, there's the final irony!" His voice was caustic. "Now that I know? Nothing has changed. I discovered that last night. When we sat next to each other listening to the Mozart, I knew what I had been missing all these years. What I share with you I've never had with anyone before, not even in the early days with Amanda. But I was right, there's a price to pay for that kind of love. When I saw you in Michel's arms on the dance floor, I knew how important you really were to me and how vulnerable I had become."

"And you were furious with me, weren't you?"

"Only for a moment. I'd realized before I'd even reached the street that in no way were you like Amanda." He suddenly leaned over and kissed her. "Oh, my darling, don't look at me like that!" Reluctantly he let his hands slide from her shoulders and sat back. "No," he continued after a moment. "The problem was never you. It's me. How can I ask you to share my life, a life that may include such bursts of insane jealousy and suspicion? No—" he put his fingers on her lips "—don't answer too quickly. Be truthful, Connie. You're so honest and open, and I feel so guarded and mistrustful. Could you bear to share that kind of life?"

She replied without hesitation. "No, but I don't expect to live that kind of life with you." Her eyes were bright with love and faith. "Don't you remember—I'm the one with confidence."

"And I'm the one in whom it's been killed by experience."

Impulsively she put her hands on his shoulders and said, "Can't you see that your being able to tell me all this shows that you *do* have confidence—in life and in me? Trust is something you can only get back by taking a chance again. Make the leap and see, George!"

He caught her to him in a sudden surge of passion. "Oh, Connie," he murmured, "I only know that I love you, and that I hadn't thought I would say that to anyone ever again."

As she lay in his arms, she felt his lips move down her throat and along her shoulders, toward the rose nestling in the curve of her breasts. A delicious lassitude overtook her, as if her blood had turned to honey. Yet as his hands passed lightly and lingeringly over her body, she responded to him eagerly, her ardor matching his. As he removed the rose, her hand found the top button of her dress and she began to help him.

What seemed like a hundred tolling bells brought Connie to her senses. Every church in the area was ringing out the noon hour.

"Oh, George," Connie gasped, "I had no idea it was so late! I promised Miss Levering I'd be back for lunch."

George looked at her in disbelief, then regretfully released her from his embrace. His eyes still heavy with desire, he asked softly, "Can't Miss Levering wait, Connie?"

"It's not Miss Levering that's important, George. It's that I promised. I don't want to go, I really don't. But I must. Please understand."

As he rose in one agile movement, she sat up and held out her hands to him. Pulling her to her feet, he kept her a moment at arm's length before he drew her to him and lightly kissed the top of her head.

"I understand that I love you enough even to take you back now—and that, my love, is not the easiest thing I've ever had to do!"

Connie was reassured by the hint of laughter in his voice. "I love you, George. There'll be other times for us. And if you'll make that leap, there can be a lifetime of them."

Her eyes begged for an answer, but he said nothing as hand in hand they walked back across the open meadow to the car.

Despite Cynthia Levering's dire predictions, the evening was a great success. Pervenche's delivery of "The Grasshopper and the Ant" revealed a dramatic side of her heretofore unsuspected. The songs and dances that Connie had coached the girls in went without a hitch. But by common agreement the real triumph was Connie's acting in the love scene from *No Trifling with Love*. In the afterglow from her morning with George, Connie performed with a fire and passion that brought the audience to its feet and surprised even Michel. As they took their bows, he gallantly kissed her hand and whispered, "You were magnificent, *ma belle*. And tonight life for us must imitate art."

She smiled. Michel, she knew, had misinterpreted her fervor, seeing in it proof that he had finally won her. How ruffled he would be if he knew that it was George who had inspired her, George whose eyes she sought out even now, and in whose gaze she could read nothing but delight, as though he were rejoicing in her triumph. A sense of relief coursed through her, and she realized that she had been worried about his response. It was clear that she needn't have been concerned.

"Come. Let's get some champagne." Taking her firmly by the arm, Michel whisked Connie into the dining room, where a magnificent buffet was spread out on the long refectory table. Whether because of the heat or his exhilaration, Michel was quickly downing two glasses of champagne to everyone else's one, and their effect was obvious by the time Martine, who had not bothered to be present for the performance, swept into the room on the arm of an affluent-looking man whom she brought over and introduced as Monsieur Lavalle, from Lyons.

"Not Lavalle of Lavalle Silks?" Michel asked with a knowing smile.

"At your service, monsieur," the other replied coldly.

Michel turned to Martine, who was already on storm

alert, and, ignoring her warning glances, he winked broadly and said, "Nice going, Martine. You don't waste much time in regrets, do you?"

"You're drunk, Michel," she answered disdainfully. "Come, Charles. Let's get something to eat." She led Lavalle away, passing as she did George and Diana, to whom she gave a pleasant nod. Martine was not one to bear any ill will, particularly now that she had her sights set elsewhere.

"You were wonderful," said George, looking directly at Connie.

"Ah. A compliment from the moody Mr. Trevelyan should be treasured. The fact is," Michel said with an insinuating look, "Connie is an apt pupil. She needs only the right kind of coaching to bring her out."

"Coaching has nothing to do with it, Chevigny, and you're a fool if you think so," George said smoothly as he turned away to address Pervenche, who had just joined the group.

"Mademoiselle Harvitte, I've known you for years, and I never suspected you had such talent. I enjoyed your performance enormously."

Pervenche's answering smile showed that she was reconsidering her opinion of George.

Michel, impatient with this byplay, suddenly reached for Connie's hands. "I have to talk to you."

"Can't it wait till tomorrow, Michel?"

"It'll just take a minute. Come, Connie, it's important."

Connie shrugged and allowed Michel to lead her from the dining room into the garden.

No sooner were they there than without a word, Michel lunged at her, groping at the low scoop-neck of the embroidered peasant blouse she had worn as a costume.

"Michel, you must be out of your mind! What are you doing?"

"I've had enough of your virginal little games," he said drunkenly. "You couldn't have acted as well as you did tonight if you hadn't been attracted to me. A blind man could have seen that you were in love."

Connie didn't know if she should laugh or scream for help. Michel was being ridiculous, but, on the other hand, he was surprisingly strong, and she found she was unable to break away from him.

"Let go of her, Chevigny." George's voice, dangerously quiet, carried softly through the sultry night. Michel was too drunk to care.

"That sounds like Trevelyan the spoilsport," he said, sneering. "Too bad, Trevelyan, but I've won the lady!"

An arm reached out of the darkness and effortlessly whirled Michel around like a puppet. "You've had too much to drink," George said contemptuously. "Go get some black coffee and sober up. *Now*, Chevigny, *now*, before I help you on your way!"

Michel looked at him stupidly for a moment, then at Connie; his face showed a slowly dawning comprehension. "You mean it's real?" He turned to Connie. "You really love him, Connie?"

"Yes, Michel, with all my heart."

"Trevelyan?"

"For God's sake, leave us alone, Chevigny!"

"I didn't realize," Michel said, suddenly sober. "I've played the role often enough to recognize it, though." His voice was bemused. "All right, Trevelyan, far be it from me to interfere with true love. God knows it's rare enough."

He began to stumble toward the house, but after a few steps he looked back at Connie and said, "And yet, what a pity."

As they watched his uncertain departure, Connie

sent George a telepathic message: *Have confidence. Make the leap. Make the leap.*

She could barely see him, though she knew he was close. Tall, lean, his hands in his pockets, he was a presence, a force. The tension was unbearable. When he finally spoke, it was to ask casually, "Would you like to know what I did this afternoon?"

Whatever Connie had expected to hear, it was not this. She felt deflated by disappointment. She had dared too much.

"I've been quite busy," he continued, as if he had gotten an answer. Then he laughed that wonderful boyish laugh she had heard only once before. Just then the moon broke through the clouds and flooded the garden with silvery light. "Oh, Connie, if you could only see your face! It's all right, darling, it's all right!" His voice was regretful. "I shouldn't have teased you—but I *have* been busy, darling. I've been learning to leap."

Still Connie was silent.

One long step took him to her. His voice was excited, vibrant. "Connie, I've been on the phone all afternoon. We can be in Paris tomorrow night, and we can be married Monday morning. There's only one thing." He hesitated. "I couldn't find the right kind of ring here in Aix. Will you wear this until we can choose one together?"

He handed Connie a small velvet box.

When she made no move to open it, she saw George's face harden.

"Connie? Connie, why don't you say something? Have you changed your mind?"

"Oh, George, never that! It's just that I love you so much I'm afraid to believe that this is happening."

Without a word he took the box from her and opened it. A heavy gold chain gleamed in the moonlight, and on it was George's moonstone ring. Carefully he placed it around her neck, his fingers caressing her lovingly. Then with a mischievous grin he said, "I guess you'll just have to make the leap and see!"

Laughing, she melted into his arms, and he stilled that laughter with a passionate kiss.